One of the rentboys, a good-looking fellow dressed in pale grey and casually smoking a cigarette, stood before him. In a well-modulated and carefully accented voice, the boy spoke quietly. 'Looking for someone?' The boy was positioned across the street, actually some distance away, with crowds and vehicles passing between the two of them. But to Oscar his voice sounded intimate and very close by, as if it were whispering in his ear.

Oscar wanted to turn away, to ignore the lad, but the handsome rentboy looked at him so knowingly, so openly, that Oscar couldn't for a moment so much as move. It was ridiculous, of course, impossible, but something in the youth's vitality, his brazen eye, struck Oscar as palpably as if a giant fist had hit him squarely in the forehead.

The easy camaraderie he had always enjoyed with younger men was an admitted fact, but there was something happening here that did not fit the mould Oscar sought. His breathing came with difficulty, and his heart would not stop pounding. He was suddenly frightened, for himself, for Constance and Cyril, and the new baby on the way ...

Stefan Rudnicki is an actor, producer and award-winning playwright. He has directed more than 130 theatre productions and is the author of three actor's resource books and an adaptation of Sun Tzu's The Art of War. He is co-author of Colin Powell and the American Dream.

THE NOVEL

Stefan Rudnicki

Based on the screenplay by Julian Mitchell

ORION

An Orion paperback
First published in 1997 by
Orion Books Limited
Orion House, 5 Upper St Martin's Lane
London WC2H 9EA

A CIP catalogue record for this book is available
from the British Library

ISBN: 0 75281 160 6

Typeset by Deltatype Limited, Birkenhead, Merseyside
Printed and bound in Great Britain by
Clays Ltd, St Ives plc

ACKNOWLEDGEMENTS

Thanks to the people without whose assistance and support this book could not have been written: Michael Viner and Deborah Raffin of Dove Entertainment for the opportunity to embark upon the journey; Mark Aarons, Beth Lieberman, and Steve Baeck at Dove Books; Caroline Oakley at Orion, whose initial editorial comments helped shape the book; Colleen Platt for her exhaustive and authoratitive notes; Roger Rees for bringing the book to life so brilliantly on audio; Peter Samuelson for his role as communicator and facilitator. I wish especially to thank Julian Mitchell for his brilliant screenplay and the team that brought it to life as a truly exceptional motion picture: producers Peter and Marc Samuelson, director Brian Gilbert, Stephen Fry – who is Oscar Wilde – Vanessa Redgrave, Jennifer Ehle, Jude Law, and the rest of a wondrous cast.

A film novelisation is, at best, a hybrid of forms. When the film is based on actual events and real people – persons whose actions are to this day controversial – serious issues of authenticity and points of views arise. It has been my intention in writing this to be diligently true to the dramatic, emotional and political thrust of the film. This has meant that key elements of Wilde's life – especially his relationships with other notables of the time like Aubrey

Beardsley, Pierre Louys, Lillie Langtry and André Gide — are not even alluded to. In other instances, liberty has been taken in matters of strict chronology, location and character detail. No biographical film can be made without such departures from what may be accepted as 'true history'. The field must be narrowed and a clear posture maintained. This book is not a biography, but a work of fiction, inspired by an important and eloquent motion picture. If I have managed to approach even occasionally that importance and that eloquence, I shall consider the exercise a success.

I refer those readers who wish to delve further into the detail and scope of Oscar Wilde's world — as I hope all will — to the biographies by Frank Harris and Richard Ellman, and, of course, to the writings of Oscar Wilde himself.

POLYGRAM FILMED ENTERTAINMENT

present

a Samuelson Production in association with Dove
International Inc NDF International Ltd/Pony Canyon Inc
Pandora Film Capitol Films and BBC Films with the
participation of The Greenlight Fund
A Brian Gilbert Film

Stephen Fry Jude Law Vanessa Redgrave Jennifer Ehle

WILDE

Gemma Jones Judy Parfitt Michael Sheen
Zoe Wanamaker Tom Wilkinson

Casting Director Sarah Bird Editor Michael Bradsell
Production Designer Maria Djurkovic Costume Designer
Nic Ede Director of Photography Martin Fuhrer Sound
Mixer Jim Greenhorn Line Producer Nick O'Hagan
Music Composed and Conducted by Debbie Wiseman
Executive Producers Michiyo Yoshizaki Michael Viner
Deborah Raffin Alex Graham Alan Howden Original
Screenplay by Julian Mitchell from "Oscar Wilde" by
Richard Ellman Produced by Marc Samuelson and Peter
Samuelson Directed by Brian Gilbert.

www.oscarwilde.com

SAMUELSON PRODUCTIONS

Kodak

ORION
MEDIA

PROLOGUE

*We have really everything in common
with America nowadays, except, of
course, language.*

A SPRAY OF FINE, powdery dust blossomed into the
windless, hazy afternoon sky, hanging there for several
seconds before settling back on to the narrow dirt track, the
low brush which dotted the earth in unkept fashion and
was for many miles its sole vegetation, and the barely
visible lizard watching from a boulder a few yards off.
Riders and horses, all three pairs of them, were quickly
gone, but the syncopated confusion of their passing
hoofbeats rang on in the still air and echoed through the
empty passages under the dry crust of the land. When all
was still again, the lizard, covered by a further layer of
camouflaging dust, became wholly invisible.

On a bluff overlooking the barely discernible track, a
lookout spotted the approaching riders and halloed to
another lookout just about a gunshot away. That lookout
called to yet another, and so the news spread that the
visitor, moving more slowly and thus still out of sight, was
on his way, and that one and all should gather.

And gather they did that fine thirteenth day of April in 1882 in Leadville, Colorado.

They could hardly see for the dust. They could hardly hear for the din. They could hardly even stand for the jostling of their neighbours, nearly a hundred men, young and old, and a few women. More people, perhaps, than had ever gathered for anything there.

It wasn't much of a crowd by cosmopolitan standards, but then Leadville wasn't much of a town either; just a single unpaved track, barely a street, leading up a hillside to a mine. A pair of broad, ostentatious two-storey buildings dominated the street. Their ornate wooden balconies and stained glass dwarfed the uneven rows of shacks and tents that housed the mine's accoutrements and the majority of the town's population. Shiny tin roofs showed patches of rust, reminders of the early spring rains and runoff that were already history to the parched land.

But the dry spell was nearly at an end. Leadville was about to be visited by an unparalleled aesthetic munificence. The anticipation was keen, the excitement nearly unbearable. The shacks, the weighing shed and the sluicing creek were abandoned. The great vista of mountains stretching to a far horizon was ignored. The silver mine had come to a dead halt, as everyone crowded along the track leading to the pit works.

A scattered chorus of 'Where is he?' bounced about the crowd.

Then a shout, 'Here he is!'

Head and shoulders above the throng, a curious figure came floating towards the mine. He was a giant of a man, dressed in a long green coat with fur collar and cuffs offset by a miner's black slouch hat. His shirt had a wide Byronic collar and he wore a sky-blue tie. Rings glistened on his fingers, and a cigarette, held a little away from his body as if it were a wand of power or a rod of empire, sent easy plumes of contrasting ash-white smoke into the cobalt Colorado air.

He was riding a mule, being led along by members of his welcoming party, a slightly deferential self-appointed retinue: the sheriff, the owner of the Leadville Hotel, and the manager of the town's theatre, the Tabor Grand Opera House. They basked in reflected light, the attention they were getting just from being with such a famous man.

Like royalty among his subjects, he acknowledged the crown with a genial wave, inspiring applause and crude cries of, 'Hey, Oscar! Oscar!'

Oscar Wilde beamed, and took off his hat in salute.

There was a robust familiarity in these shouts. It was as if the visitor from abroad had suddenly been sworn in as a member of this great family that was America without benefit of marriage or adoption, those modern social rituals that bring people of radically diverse backgrounds together.

He was in the fourth month of his year-long American lecture tour. He was a young man, only twenty-seven and a half years old, and his enormous vitality was evident to all. He was yet to write those fabulous plays, the novel and the children's stories that were to make him a legendary literary figure. But even without benefit of *oeuvre*, he was an international celebrity, propelled to instant fame by his brash and cutting wit and the publicity surrounding the D'Oyly Carte Opera Company's production of Gilbert and Sullivan's *Patience*. The operetta's leading character, Bunthorne, was modelled after Wilde, and successful productions in London, and subsequently in New York, gave a decided boost to Oscar's already growing notoriety. The company's owner, Richard D'Oyly Carte, also ran a lecture circuit, and had approached Wilde about a tour which might, as one journalist suggested, set Wilde's 'hyper-aestheticism ... as an antidote to America's hyper-materialism'.

Having already crossed the continent from New York to San Francisco, Oscar was no stranger to Americans and their geographical and social landscapes. But Leadville set a new standard for wilderness, and Oscar had to work harder than usual to maintain his composure. A location more desolate was difficult to imagine, even for one initiated to the travails of the colonial lecture circuit.

Looking around from atop his mule, Oscar could see distant vistas that seemed to span the continent itself. At the same time, he was overwhelmed by the shouts and the smells and the hundred little colourful details of the humanity around him. Face after face turned up to him, and presented a new and different aspect. He swam a sea of minutiae; an eye, a nose, a missing tooth, a crease in someone's forehead, a knife scar, a disfigured ear ... all passing by him against the backdrop of mountains and sky.

Oscar suddenly experienced a bewildering loss of orientation. More than at any other time in his travels, he felt swept along on a tide that left him powerless. He knew himself incapable of halting the stream, or of changing to the smallest degree the direction of his journey. Even his keen analytical wit had, for the moment, left him, as he bumped along on the mule, uncomprehending, dazed, but feeling more, it seemed to him, than ever before in his life. 'Somewhere and sometime,' he muttered to himself, 'and I am not sure where or when.' Curiously, and against all logic, he found that he enjoyed the sensation very much.

Waiting at the head of the mineshaft, next to the large rickety bucket by which miners travelled up and down the shaft, was a further welcoming committee, led in stature and authority by the owner of the mine. As the man stepped forward, he seemed to Oscar self-aware, almost shy, clearly unused to formal occasions and speaking to groups.

'Hello, sir,' the man began. 'You are most welcome.' Then he raised his voice to the assembly at large. 'All right, everybody, listen up. I want to introduce you to Oscar Wilde.' He turned back to Oscar, and in the formal tones of one performing a dedication, said, 'Welcome to the Matchless Silver Mine. Today we opened a new seam. We're going to name it after you.'

Oscar was helped off the mule, and his renewed contact with terra firma helped clear his head. He nodded graciously, 'How very kind. I look forward to collecting the royalties.'

This was a sample of Oscar's legendary wit, a preliminary salvo calculated to test the audience. He was pleased to see that his quip went down very well, as a burst of appreciative applause almost drowned out the mine own-er's next remark.

'Now, why don't you follow me over here . . .' he invited, gesturing.

Oscar, to hear better, leaned in over the shaft, seeing the bucket and the darkness below. The alarm he felt, a split-second of stiffness, was quickly subdued, and no one saw.

While the bucket was held in place, Oscar stepped into it. Gingerly, but with great panache, he thought.

With a fierce burst of energy from the miners, the bucket

was at once hauled up into the air, where it swung dizzyingly for a few moments. Oscar reigned, demigod above the common throng below.

The common throng approved.

Oscar doffed his hat in another gracious salute.

In sudden impromptu gestures of response, a couple of dozen hats from the crowd were tossed into the air. Cheers rang out.

And then he was gone.

The hubbub of the crowd quickly faded to a faint echo, as Oscar hurtled downwards through almost pitch darkness, the bucket clanking and banging against the sides of the shaft, the chains from which it hung creaking dismally. The heart-arresting descent, in reality much slower than it appeared to him, seemed to go on and on, until the bucket arrived at the bottom with a bump.

Terrified nearly senseless by the fall and the apparently impenetrable darkness around him, Oscar nevertheless felt stirrings of emotion in his breast akin to a profound and unaccountable joy. It was as if the bucket ride had jarred loose some fragment of his soul that could now range abroad in new-found freedom.

As his eyes adjusted, Oscar was able to distinguish the party of miners waiting to greet him. They were young and tough. It was hot down here in the pit of the silver mine, and many of the men were stripped to the waist. All were covered in dirt and streaked with sweat. The only light came from their kerosene lamps and candles, highlighting the rippling sheen of muscle and the sparkle of eye.

The miners looked at Oscar in silence.

He stepped out of the bucket, and looked carefully and slowly around.

'I thought I was descending into hell.' Oscar breathed a sigh, trying to capture the miners and the moment. 'But with these angel faces to greet me – it must be paradise.'

There was no reaction whatever from the miners. Oh yes, they were paying attention all right. Their eyes were on him, and they seemed to be listening very hard in the preternatural stillness of the cavern. But he could not read them. Then, as if by silent mutual consent, a stirring of activity and the beginnings of movement.

'Is this the way to my personal seam?' asked Oscar as the men began to lead him down the tunnel, further into the bowels of the mine. 'Of course, I should have preferred gold. Purple and gold. But we live in a silver age, alas.'

Again, there was no laughter, no comment from the men, who were much too serious about protecting their charge to allow humour a foothold, even if they did comprehend the joke.

Although the heat was oppressive, the air foul, and the darkness a palpable presence waiting just beyond their feeble lights to engulf them, the walk was not long, and, for Oscar, it was made more bearable by the presence of one young man in particular. He was slim and good-looking, his name was Jones, and he had assumed Oscar as his personal charge. Something about him, a solicitous manner and a twinkling eye perhaps, provided encouragement, and suggested to Oscar that, if this Hades was lacking a Persephone, there might yet be other attractions.

Some minutes later, they arrived at their destination, a large area of excavation, a wound in the earth propped open by massive strategically placed wooden beams. The silver seam glistened in the rock.

As if a signal had been given, the miners found places to

sit against the rock face, an informal audience perhaps five rows deep. They broke out a couple of bottles of whiskey and began their 'supper', passing the bottle from one to another, gazing with unconcealed innocence and awe at Oscar. Several of the men led him to a seat of honour on a raised platform of stone, and offered him the even greater honour of a mug to drink from.

Oscar spoke to them, casually but with authority. Although his views on the aesthetics of life, art and dress, as expressed in his prepared lecture on 'The House Beautiful' seemed to range far afield from the more immediate concerns of the company, Oscar knew from previous experience that they would glean more than he could possibly have anticipated. These miners, like so many other audiences Oscar had addressed in America, looked to him for a special kind of nourishment. They were like children, eager to be shown glimpses of a sensitivity and awareness to which they could barely aspire. They came away from Oscar's attacks on materialistic vulgarity with a vision of what they might yet become, and if, in the process, they had to hear how bad they were, the attention pleased them and made them feel somehow more important for the abuse.

And they gave Oscar something back as well. Reflected in the innocence of his American children, Oscar could see the growing power of his vision. Their open naturalness was antithetical to the self-conscious artifice he espoused but, rather than finding their barbarism abhorrent, Oscar found himself sustained by their adulation of him and by their willingness to change. As he observed the impact of his words on audiences across America, he was able fully to comprehend in practice the principle that had been until then only theory: that life, and the lives of those he reached, would indeed imitate the art that he brought to them.

'So much that is exquisitely beautiful is wrought from suffering,' Oscar stated mildly, easily finding a common thread to tie the miners to him, 'from pain, from toil, from hardship, from broken bones and blistered skin. Emeralds, rubies, opals, gold and, of course, silver. Benvenuto Cellini, he understood silver. He took the metal you mine so nobly down here and transformed it into works of art for popes and princes. The salt-cellar he made for the king of France, for example, is a miracle of workmanship.'

They were warming to Oscar now. Grunts of agreement and sighs of comprehension filled the dense air of the mine, and a voice echoed, 'Cellini? Is he a wop?'

Oscar peered out and found the miner responsible for the question before responding genially. 'A Renaissance man. In every sense. The greatest silversmith the world has ever seen. And a genius in life as well as art. He experimented with every vice known to man, he committed murder, he . . .'

'He killed a man?' Oscar saw Jones lean forward eagerly. The young man had apparently found something he could understand and celebrate.

'More than one,' Oscar answered.

With the directness and cordiality Oscar had found common among many Americans, Jones stood. In two quick strides, he was filling Oscar's mug. He seemed comfortable with this as well.

'Thank you,' Oscar said gently.

Jones's smile lit up even the dimmest corners of the mine. As he returned to his place among the other miners,

Jones raised the bottle in a toast, 'Hey, you're a bully-boy, Oscar!'

Out of the chorus of agreement, another miner's voice called, 'I'd like to meet this Cellini. Why didn't you bring him with you?'

'I'm afraid he's dead,' said Oscar.

Without missing a beat, Jones asked, 'Who shot him?'

To this Oscar had no reply. He merely tilted his head to one side in profoundly genial amusement.

CHAPTER 1

London, 1883

Women are a decorative sex. They never have anything to say, but they say it charmingly. Women represent the triumph of matter over mind, just as men represent the triumph of mind over morals.

REFLECTIONS ON THE American tour from which he had recently returned tumbled about in Oscar's head as the open cab stopped abruptly in front of his mother's house near Grosvenor Square. He breathed in his full and present appreciation of the fine London afternoon. It was early autumn, but many trees had already turned, and the yellow leaves fluttering every which way in the brisk breeze appealed to Oscar's penchant for the pale hues of autumn, so much less vulgar than the abundant verdure of summer.

He descended from the cab, and smiled as he handed the handsome young cabman a note.

'Keep the change.'

'Thank you very much. Mr Wilde.'

'Recklessness should always be rewarded. And you drove so fast, I felt like the sun god at the mercy of young Phaeton.'

'This isn't a phaeton, sir,' said the puzzled cabman, referring to the carriage model. 'It's a victoria.'

'The dear Queen-Empress would have felt even more exalted than I did. But really, you should drive a hansom,' said Oscar catching the cabman's grin just out of the corner of his eye. As the cab drove away, Oscar stood for a moment on the threshold. He hesitated before knocking on his mother's door, always a daunting proposition.

Despite the cheeriness of this particularly beautiful late afternoon, evening gloom possessed the inside of the house.

Born Jane Elgee, Speranza Francesca Wilde was a woman who, like her son, enjoyed improving upon reality, and reinvented herself several times in her life. Having dismissed plain Jane, in favour of a questionable Italian heritage and fierce Irish patriotism, she wore her husband's knighthood well, choosing in recent years to be identified simply as Speranza, Lady Wilde.

William Robert Wilde, a physician of some brilliance who had received the great honour of being appointed Surgeon Oculist to the Queen, had died seven years earlier, a broken man in the wake of a baroque sex scandal. In 1864 a patient of his, Mary Travers, wrote accusatory letters to the newspapers suggesting that William had raped her a couple of years earlier. A protesting letter Speranza wrote to the woman's father, a newly-appointed professor of jurisprudence at Trinity College, propelled Travers to sue Lady Wilde for libel. Although Mary Travers was clearly not an innocent in the matter, William was found to be not without blame either, and had to bear the burden of £2,000 in costs on his wife's behalf.

William left Speranza two sons, Willie and Oscar, and the sweet memory of their daughter Isola, who had died of fever when she was nine. He also left her an estate insufficient to support the family.

Although not at all well off, Speranza was unwilling to curtail her salon and other social activities, so she had taken to dimming her world in the hope that others might not notice how hopelessly out of fashion it was. The curtains were drawn, and the small sitting-room, papered in crimson with gold stars, was lit by red-shaded candles. Mirrors were strategically hung to confuse the senses and give the illusion of rooms beyond rooms in ever-retreating dim splendour.

Speranza was now in her late fifties, tall and big-boned like Oscar, and very eccentric in dress. That day she sported a ten-year-old dress from her days as a Dublin hostess, and wore her hair down her back. Her ever-active, dancing hands and her distinctly Irish accent dominated the 'at home' she was hosting.

Speranza's tea was execrable, but the infectious incandescence of her personality and the abundance of sensational gossip brought people flocking, and many of her guests were regulars at these events.

As he entered, Oscar was pleased to see Ada Leverson, a clever writer with a feline manner, who had recently become a great friend. She was accompanied by her husband, Ernest Leverson, a pleasant enough man of inherited wealth, deficient business skills and a passion for gambling. Also present was Georgina Tollemache, Lady Mount-Temple, a widow whose political connections and strongly expressed opinions rendered her a mainstay of the social season. Oscar's attentions, however, were drawn to Constance Lloyd, a rather serious young woman with great coils of chestnut hair who was related to friends of the Wildes in Ireland.

Soon Oscar and Constance were chatting intimately in a corner of the room, while Speranza and Ada looked on.

'Is Miss Lloyd connected to Lloyd's Bank?' asked Ada.

'No,' replied Speranza.

'Pity.'

'But she's comfortable, Ada. A thousand a year.'

'Then I congratulate you, Lady Wilde. Now that Oscar has been to America and sown his Wildean oats, it's time he settled down.'

Constance was three years Oscar's junior, with strong interests in all the fashionable pursuits: music, painting, embroidery and Italian literature, Dante in particular. In public she tended to appear withdrawn, but with Oscar she came into her own. Today as usual, in their corner apart, she played the ever-attentive listener, encouraging with just the right question, look or gesture.

'But weren't they very rough?' she inquired.

'No, no, charming.' said Oscar. 'Well, charming to me. With each other, it's true, they could be a little brusque. They hanged two men in the theatre one night, just before I gave my lecture. I felt like the sorbet after a side of beef.'

Not knowing whether to believe him or not, Constance was nevertheless very taken with Oscar's story. Her gentle, musical laugh complemented Oscar's perfectly, a harmony to which he was not deaf. From time to time Oscar would catch a glimpse of Constance and himself in a mirror, and he found the pair to be attractive, her deference, intelligence and shyness a most pleasing contrast to his flamboyant manner. She brought out in him a watchful solicitude that he interpreted as a new-found maturity, which he also found attractive.

Others had doubts about the match and, in the shifting configuration of such social events, Lady Mount-Temple found herself beside Ada, from which vantage she peered at Oscar through her glass.

'I know your friend is famous, Ada. Notorious, at least. But I cannot understand for what.'

Gazing fondly at Oscar, Ada replied, 'For being himself, Lady Mount-Temple.'

This was not a savoury recommendation to Lady Mount-Temple, who proceeded to study the couple with a kind of ferocity, as Constance and Oscar, unaware of her scrutiny, continued their conversation.

'I read in the paper,' said Constance, 'that you said there was too much ornament everywhere.'

'There is.' Oscar smiled, then reflected a moment. 'All really ugly things are made by people trying to make something beautiful. And all beautiful ones by people trying to make something useful.'

Constance paused, impressed by Oscar's authority and seriousness. 'Don't Americans talk the most wonderful slang, though?'

'Well, I did hear one lady say, "After the heel-lick I shifted my day goods."'

'What on earth did she mean?'

'She meant that she'd changed her clothes after an afternoon dance.'

Constance laughed, and Oscar continued. 'The Americans

have a very refreshing way with the language. But dear Constance, you'll never talk like that, will you? Promise?'

Her light laughter fading to a gentle smile. Constance was about to promise much more, when their intimacy was interrupted by the approach of Speranza. She quickly pulled Constance away, sweeping her across the room to Lady Mount-Temple for a formal introduction.

'Connie, my love,' said Speranza, positively bouncing with excitement. 'Lady Mount-Temple is so anxious to meet you.'

'I knew your father, Miss Lloyd.' Lady Mount-Temple pronounced. 'I am sorry to hear you have lost him.'

She made this sound almost as though it was Constance's fault.

'If you knew him, you must have liked him, Lady Mount-Temple,' replied Constance. 'Everyone did.'

Lady Mount-Temple smiled benignly, for the moment allowing Constance the benefit of the doubt.

Ada observed the exchange with a Sphinx-like smile. Oscar, now by her side, seemed more at ease, as if a mask had dropped. With her he could indulge his foremost social passion, that of observing others and commenting on them. In this pastime, Ada's honest perception and dry wit made her his favourite companion. He employed a light, self-mocking tone rarely heard by others as he nodded in Constance's direction.

'She's delightful. And not stupid – really, not stupid at all.'

Ada, her smile still fixed, asked, 'Is that quite a reason to marry her?'

'Well, I must marry someone. And my mother has our

future planned out in every detail. I'm to go into Parliament.'

You'll be standing as a Reform candidate, I assume,' said Ada archly. 'Dress Reform, that is.'

At this Oscar laughed, but the laugh rang a bit hollow and soon faded. He felt overwhelmed by the dreary surroundings, by Speranza's salon, and by the vistas of political accomplishment and unbounded domesticity which suddenly seemed to stretch before him with terrifying inevitability. He became abruptly grave and most serious.

'We're to have a nice house, and live a proper settled life. Literature and lectures and the House of Commons — receptions for the world in general at five o'clock ...'

'How dreary!' commented Ada.

'Your attendance will not be required at those. But your sphinxiness will be essential to our intimate little dinners at eight,' continued Oscar, suddenly breaking into a sing-song Irish lilt that was a shockingly accurate imitation of his mother. ''Twill be a *grand* life, a *charming* life.'

Ada looked at him thoughtfully. 'I see Constance will be busy preparing the dinners. But what will she contribute to the literature and lectures?'

'She will correct the proofs of my articles,' replied Oscar smugly.

'Oh, what a little sunbeam!' quipped Ada.

Oscar lit a cigarette for Ada, then one for himself. His mood and tone shifted quite rapidly, as he turned serious again.

'I do love her, Ada. She's ...'

And, for once, Oscar simply couldn't find the words. He could not, even to Ada, explain the particular appeal that

Constance, dreary vistas notwithstanding, held for him. Were she to become his, a special light would grace his life for ever, and a jewel of no small substance would ornament his being. There was indeed something almost American in her innocence.

'Silent,' said Ada, 'I find her very silent.'

'But so sympathetic,' said Oscar. 'And I do need an audience.'

They laughed together at this, but Oscar's laugh was a trifle forced.

CHAPTER 2

*A mother's love is very touching, of
course, but it is often curiously selfish.*

TWO YEARS HAD passed.

It was a fine morning, and sunlight dazzled from the
windows of the grand buildings where many barristers and
solicitors had their offices. Oscar strode along, hat off to the
sun, swinging his cane and sporting a buttonhole. His hair
was shorter now, since his marriage, and he wore it waved.
He was humming to himself and feeling very pleased with
life. Even the tide of lawyers in wigs and gowns moving
toward him proved no obstacle. The sea merely parted,
with some turning of heads, to let Oscar through.

There was no stopping Oscar this day, as he proceeded
from Charing Cross station up the Strand and then down
Fleet Street. He was on his way to work, his mind fixed, on
a mission of utmost historical importance.

Oscar's gifts, exemplified by the literary reviews he wrote
for several periodicals, but chiefly the *Pall Mall Gazette*, had
attracted attention from, among others George Bernard
Shaw and, more importantly at the time, Thomas Wemyss
Reid, the general manager of Cassell & Company, publisher

of a new magazine entitled *The Lady's World: A Magazine of Fashion and Society*. Oscar was asked to recommend improvements to the magazine, and his success led to his appointment as editor. His destination that day was the magazine's offices in Ludgate Hill.

After taking the stairs two at a time, Oscar burst into the office, where a dozen or so people were at work, preparing the next issue. They looked up as Oscar entered.

'Good morning, good morning!' His energy was infectious. 'Your editor has made a radical decision. As the next century will be the century of Art, and women have a natural instinct for what is artistic ...' Oscar paused for the expected laugh. 'Women will be the vanguard of the new sensibility. To be the leading advocate for what is artistic and womanly, our journal must be all-embracing and democratic. From our next issue, therefore, we are changing our name from *The Lady's World* to ...'

With his flair for the dramatic, Oscar let them wait, timing his announcement to the precise moment for greatest effect.

'*The* Woman's *World!*' he finished.

There was a silence as the staff stared at him, not sure whether he was serious or not.

He beamed round, delighted with their confusion, before continuing.

'One only has to be born a lady. To be a woman is a real achievement. Now our readers will be the whole nation of British womanhood. Led by dear Queen Victoria, whom I have asked, as a feeling and suffering woman, to contribute a poem.'

At this there was more silence, then a brief scattering of scandalised laughter.

'I posted the letter on my way to the underground railway this morning.' Oscar smiled at one and all. 'It was my work for the day, the rest of which I have set aside to be with my wife, who is both a lady and a woman.'

Oscar put his hat back on, and, with a cheery 'Good morning!' left the office and its array of gaping mouths.

Oscar's social circle had grown rapidly. The thought of standing for Parliament, albeit Speranza's idea, briefly attracted him. His marriage made that sort of life seem within reach and eminently desirable.

In 1884, he had negotiated a lease on a house at 16 Tite Street in Chelsea. He asked his friend the American painter James A. McNeill Whistler to decorate the house, but when Whistler turned him down saying, 'No, Oscar, you have been lecturing to us about the House Beautiful; now is your chance to show us one,' Oscar turned to Edward Godwin, an architect destined to achieve a measure of notoriety for his love affair with the renowned actress Ellen Terry. Rejecting the ornate Pre-Raphaelite detail and William Morris wallpapers which had characterised Oscar's previous habitation — also in Tite Street — Godwin intended that the house set a new standard in interior design.

Oscar had agreed to everything, seeking a brighter, more open setting than had been his wont. It was especially important to him to shake off every last vestige of the gloom that dominated his mother's house. He needed to see inspiration everywhere he looked. Whether he was at supper, or writing, or performing his morning ablutions, it was essential that the most casual glance in any direction fall upon an object or vista of sufficient beauty to excite the brain to imaginative heights.

Tite Street was a household of oddly contrasting styles and sensibilities, mostly featuring white and off-white high-gloss enamel, with gold, blue and green highlights. His library, decorated with Moorish overtones, sported an inscription from Shelley:

> Spirit of Beauty! Tarry still awhile,
>   They are not dead, thine ancient votaries,
> Some few there are to whom thy radiant smile
>   Is better than a thousand victories.

Beneath these words, Oscar would lie on the sofa of an afternoon, reading, piles of books on the table before him and on the floor all about him. He turned the pages remarkably fast, as though skimming but not skimming at all. Completely absorbed, he did not at first hear Constance, who was thus able to enter and stand at the door watching him admiringly. As he rapidly reached the end of a chapter, Oscar looked up and smiled at her.

'I don't see how you can possibly take it all in,' she said. 'Reading at that speed.'

He held out the book to her.

'Try me.'

'I know better.'

Constance let the challenge pass, knowing that Oscar was capable of reading and retaining the salient points of a three-volume novel in half an hour. He could also sustain a conversation while reading, a skill of which he was proud and which he would demonstrate frequently.

Oscar nodded at the pile of books beside him.

'My afternoon's work.' He put his book down and

rubbed his hands thoughtfully. 'Where are we dining tonight?'

Constance moved into the room, daintily, almost coyly, her hands behind her back.

'At the Leversons'.'

'Ah, then you must show your true colours.'

Constance raised an eyebrow in alarm as Oscar looked her over, speculating on what she might wear on this occasion to demonstrate his latest excursions into fashion experiment.

'As a propagandist for dress reform,' he continued, overruling any possible protest. 'The cinnamon cashmere trousers, I think. And – the cape with the ends turned up into sleeves.'

Constance hesitated, blinking shyly.

'I ... don't think I can wear those trousers any more,' she said quietly.

Oscar hesitated, stopped more by the tone of her voice than by her words. It took him another moment to realise her meaning. Then all hesitation passed. His reaction was spontaneous, exultant. He jumped to his feet, beaming, walked to Constance, and kissed her warmly.

Then, imitating his mother, Oscar cried out, 'A new Wilde for the world? Another genius for Ireland?'

Constance nodded.

'Then we shall have to buy you a whole new wardrobe!'

Oscar embraced her with an uncommon fervour.

They held on to each other and laughed together for quite a long time, her delight a mirror of his. Oscar's idyllic household had just achieved its next level of perfection.

He pictured Constance with a baby, then with perhaps two or three children gambolling about her skirts. The issue of her wardrobe was, of course, terribly important, and he could imagine her becoming the vanguard to a whole new generation of fashionable mothers. He saw in this image a new Constance, perfected somehow, complete in a way she had never been for him before. He basked in her light.

CHAPTER 3

Life's aim, if it has one, is simply to
be always looking for temptations.
There are not nearly enough. I
sometimes pass a whole day without
coming across a single one. It is quite
dreadful. It makes one so nervous about
the future.

CYRIL PROVED TO have a happy disposition. He liked
particularly to be outdoors and, as he approached his
first birthday, his mother could be seen with increasing
frequency taking him on walks in the neighbourhood. One
day in Hyde Park, Constance was wheeling the baby in his
pram past Watt's statue of Physical Energy. Walking beside
her was Robert Ross, a small young man of seventeen,
possessed of delicate features and a very sharp intelligence.

Ada and Oscar strolled a little distance behind, in private
conversation.

'Ernest proposed to me under that statue,' said Ada.

'Really,' replied Oscar, affecting shock, 'The things that
go on in front of works of art are quite appalling. The
police should interfere.'

'Ernest's appalling people all over London. Specially me. We were made not to marry. Whereas you and Constance are so happy – everyone says so.'

'It's perfectly monstrous the way people go about nowadays, saying things behind one's back that are absolutely true.'

'So your audience has proved as responsive as you hoped?'

Oscar thought for a moment. When not speaking in jest, he wanted to be as truthful to Ada as he possibly could. She was his sounding board in this as in other matters. He could trust her to respond with equal honesty and without judging him. She was in many ways his oracle, a test of his sincerity, a sphinx without a secret agenda.

'Receptive, yes,' Oscar admitted. 'Responsive – I'm always wondering what she's really thinking.'

'I expect it's about the baby,' ventured Ada.

'You mean Robbie?' Oscar asked, eliciting a raised eyebrow from Ada. 'Yes, well ... Constance is such a natural mother, she's invited Robbie into the nest while his parents are abroad.'

Ada assumed a dubious expression, as, having closed the distance, Oscar accosted the young man.

'Robbie is Canadian,' Oscar declared, 'you can tell by his youth.'

'Have you been brought to England to mature, Mr Ross?' asked Ada, easily matching Oscar's light mocking tone without breaking stride.

'Well, that was the idea. But it doesn't seem to be working. I've lived here since I was three and you see the pitiful result.'

Ross's response had something in it of Oscar's own self-deprecating wit. Ada showed her amusement, while Constance ignored the badinage, preferring to coo to the baby. Oscar carried on effusively in a biographical vein.

'Robbie comes from a long line of imperial governors. His grandfather was Prime Minister of Upper Canada. Or was it Lower Canada? The English will take their class-system wherever they go. They apply it even to continents.'

'Are you planning to govern a continent?' Ada asked Ross.

'Oh, no. I don't even plan to govern myself,' came the reply.

Oscar looked at him, finding a sort of temptation in the youth's brash good humour and physical charm. He had perhaps the most open smile Oscar had ever seen, and a very sharp mind. Delightful, Oscar mused.

Despite his youth, Ross was hardly an innocent, and he did so fit in. Although Oscar was surprised by the strength of his feelings, it nevertheless seemed fitting that this Canadian should evoke in him a disorientation reminiscent of his American travels. He found himself remembering lines of Walt Whitman's verse and somehow longing for the lusty, full-throated song of the open road. Well, perhaps not the open road exactly. He felt suddenly confined, imprisoned by the intricately designed walks and mani-cured lawns on every side of him. It was not the road that he missed, but the singing.

Oscar turned away quickly, shielding his eyes and masking his emotions. He was not sure whether he had exposed something of his turmoil, however briefly, to Ada's sharp eye. He was also not sure that it mattered.

Oscar felt a sense of his own destiny, as though a die had been cast or a stage had been set. Only the play had not yet been written, and even the cast of characters and the nature of the drama were at best vague even to him.

As Oscar waited for his life to begin, there was still plenty to do. Shopping with and for Constance was a source of special pleasure for him, as it had been since their courtship. While Cyril stayed home in the care of his nanny, they would frequent the smarter shops, buying items singly here and there as fragments of a puzzle to be assembled later, in a household nook or on Constance's body.

Late one afternoon they were concluding their shopping in the West End. Evening was approaching with that particular low slant of light that can unexpectedly blind one for a moment. Passersby responded by either slowing down or darting recklessly about in search of a shadow. Carriages moved through the press of shoppers haltingly, horses shying to an erratic gait.

There were tarts out already, soliciting. Also rentboys, male prostitutes, looking out for potential customers. They were in their late teens and early twenties, flashy of dress and sly of eye. A particular foursome of boys loitered about, abusing the passersby with the sort of mocking comment that passed for wit among their sort.

Oscar and Constance emerged from a busy department store, she heavily pregnant again, and he very solicitous of her.

'Wait here, my dear,' Oscar said, 'I'll see if I can find a cab.' And he began to push his way through the crowd.

Then he stopped. One of the rentboys, a good-looking fellow dressed in pale grey and casually smoking a cigarette, stood before him. In a well-modulated and carefully accented voice, the boy spoke quietly. 'Looking for someone?' The boy was positioned across the street, actually some distance away, with crowds and vehicles passing between the two of them. But to Oscar his voice sounded intimate and very close by, as if it were whispering in his ear.

Oscar wanted to turn away, to ignore the lad, but the handsome rentboy looked at him so knowingly, so openly, that Oscar couldn't for a moment so much as move. It was ridiculous, of course, impossible, but something in the youth's vitality, his brazen eye, struck Oscar as palpably as if a giant fist had descended from above and struck him squarely in the forehead.

The easy camaraderie he had always enjoyed with younger men was an admitted fact, but there was something happening here that did not fit the mould that Oscar sought. His breathing came with difficulty, and his heart would not stop pounding. He was suddenly frightened, for himself, for Constance and Cyril, for the new baby on the way. Before his eyes passed a panorama of destruction. He saw the edifice of his life, which he had so carefully raised, crack and split and crumble, only to expose another image behind it: this raised eyebrow, this knowing face, this mere rentboy. Impossible.

Panicked, horrified by what he was feeling and perhaps letting it show, Oscar backed off a couple of steps, and turned, barely in control of his shaking body, ready to bolt in any direction at all, as long as it was away from the boy and that terrible knowing. Saved by a passing cab, he flagged it down as if his life depended on it.

If, in the weeks that followed, Oscar seemed a little more

distant than usual, this was ascribed by his friends and family to a critical remove appropriate to his growing reputation as a writer of literary reviews and hence an arbiter of artistic taste. The struggle that engaged his heart and soul shook his frame in private only, and his attempts to communicate his growing confusion could be only oblique and perfunctory. It was Ada Leverson who came closest to sharing Oscar's essential dilemma, but even with her there were bounds of propriety he would not cross.

Dinners at Tite Street, if not opulent, were nevertheless well-attended, and served as an important extension of Speranza's social life. After the meal, the guests would disperse into islands of observation, comment and gossip. On one such occasion, Ernest Leverson was observed showing more than a little interest in an attractive young wife, this despite the presence of a husband. Ada and Oscar were, as usual, in close conversation, observed from a distance by the now ever-present Ross.

'Perhaps it's simply the fact of living in a large cosmopolitan city,' Ada was saying. 'It's endless variety can cause restlessness.'

'And pleasure,' countered Oscar.

'London is so full of temptation for a man like Ernest,' she went on.

'For all men,' said Oscar, hesitating for fear that he might have implied too much. Glancing around, he caught Ross's watchful eye, then looked away, covering this encounter with a witticism. 'But your husband is right. One should always yield to temptation as a matter of duty. Why else is it so constantly set in one's path?'

'But if one does always yield, it becomes a habit. And habits are dreadful, surely?'

Laughing, Oscar responded, 'So dreadful, I have made a habit of not forming them.'

This was turning into a game for Oscar. How close could one come to saying something really significant without endangering privacy and reputation? All the better that there was no real danger of indiscretion on Ada's part.

'Perhaps you're not tempted so much as Ernest,' said Ada.

'Probably not. In that way, Constance is all I could ask,' said Oscar, looking about for his wife and once again catching Ross's eye. Again, he turned away, but this time more slowly and deliberately.

'Well, I am very tempted to divorce Ernest, I can tell you,' continued Ada.

Suddenly, awareness dawned upon Oscar, and Ada's plight became his sole concern.

'Oh, my poor dear Ada . . .'

Just as Ada was going to elaborate, they were interrupted by a cry from Speranza across the room.

'Oscar! Help me. Lady Mount-Temple says the English live by law and order. But I say they can't control themselves at all. You have only to look at what they've done to Ireland.'

'I refuse to discuss Ireland,' sniffed Lady Mount-Temple. 'People have been talking about it all my life, and to no purpose whatsoever.'

And as if that was all there was to be said about Ireland, Lady Mount-Temple returned to her glass of wine. Oscar, however, was not to be put off so easily, and running to his mother's defence as obliquely as possible was a technique he had mastered with long practice.

'But talk should have no purpose, Lady Mount-Temple,'

he said matter-of-factly. 'Conversation is about the fulfilment of self. It requires a personality, not a subject.'

'Fulfilment of self – what is that?' inquired Lady Mount-
Temple.

'The sole object of living,' concluded Oscar.

'Ahhh! Bravo!' cheered Speranza, clapping her hands
gleefully.

Lady Mount-Temple huffed in speechless response, while
Ross gazed at Oscar with frank admiration.

Later, Lady Mount-Temple caught up with Ada to air her
disapproval. 'He's very clever. Oscar is very clever,' she said
pointedly as they descended the stairs in their wraps.

'He's very funny, too,' added Ada.

'Perhaps I have no sense of humour. Because when he
says things like … that socialism is very conservative, I find
that irresponsible.'

'But it's true. All the radicals I know are immensely old-
fashioned.'

'I'm glad to say I know no radicals.'

'I expect you do,' countered Ada. 'But you frighten them
so much they keep their opinions to themselves.'

'There's nothing wrong with a little fear in society. It
helps keep up appearances.'

'Do appearances matter so very much?'

'They are essential,' said Lady Mount-Temple, summon-
ing up her full authority. 'If Oscar is really your friend, you
should tell him to be a little more respectful of conventional
opinion.'

'Oh, I couldn't do that,' said Ada as a parting shot. 'He'd
be so shocked.'

And they proceeded into the vestibule below where

Oscar was cheerfully saying goodbye to Ernest and the others.

Later yet, the guests gone, Constance yawned and gestured sleepily to Ross and Oscar.

'Bedtime!'

'Just one more cigarette,' Ross declared. He stepped up to the mantle and picked up an ornate carved box. Opening it, he slowly and deliberately removed a cigarette, then looked over.

'Oscar?'

'No – no thanks.'

The last thing Oscar wanted was to leave. Whatever drowsiness he felt was laced with tension. The result was a trance-like haze in which his will seemed to have been removed, leaving instead a profound lassitude through which he experienced oddly sharp twinges of sensation, both physical and emotional. Everything was enhanced for him. Every fold of fabric held mysteries in its shadows. The touch of cloth on his skin – at his neck, his wrists, the soft flesh behind his knees – alternately caressed and burned him, conveying an exquisite range of pleasurable pain. What Oscar wanted most was to examine this state at leisure and over time.

With Ross.

'Don't stay up too late, Robbie.' Constance gave Ross a motherly kiss, to which he responded with a gentle 'Good night', followed quickly with an even gentler 'Good night, Oscar.'

'Good night, Robbie,' said Oscar, and allowed himself to be led away by Constance.

Ross, left suddenly alone, placed the cigarette he had taken back in the box. He would wait.

Upstairs, Constance looked up from the new baby, Vyvyan, lying in his cot, as Oscar entered, wearing a dressing gown over his clothes. She smiled a welcome.

'Ssh! He's asleep.'

Oscar joined her over the sleeping baby.

'He's beautiful. Almost as beautiful as his mother.'

Her attention was all for the baby.

Oscar looked about the room, as if for inspiration, but all he saw was a blur of pink walls and apple-green ceiling, and the gently stirring water in Constance's bath, fragmenting the soft lamplight.

'I don't know what I'd do without you, my constant Constance.'

Oscar bent over to kiss Constance.

What began as a simple good night kiss turned, for Oscar, into something fiercely passionate. He held Constance tightly, completely enveloping her precious body in his arms, in an attempt to express the inexpressible. How could she not understand that he was adrift and that he needed her?

After some moments, he began to understand that Constance was hardly there at all. He felt her hands on his back, but without pressure, without ardour. Her lips yielded to his, but contributed nothing of herself to the kiss.

Oscar slowly released her. She stood with a light smile on her face, as if nothing had happened. And, in truth, Oscar thought, nothing had. He addressed her in the polite, formal tones appropriate to distant cousins on parting.

'Good night, my dear.'

'Good night,' said Constance as he moved away, more to the baby than to Oscar.

Leaving Constance's bedroom, Oscar shut the door behind him. He glanced down the stairs, then looked up and about. Nothing looked the same as it had even moments earlier. The house was unrecognisable to him.

As he stood there, he thought of himself as a diver, an exotic Indian diver perhaps, poised at cliff-top the moment before plunging for priceless pearls in the depths below. Then, as sensation welled up from within, Oscar understood that all firm footing was gone, that he had already leapt, and that he was in fact already falling. With this understanding came an overwhelming sense of freedom.

Oscar sighed deeply.

Then, as quietly as he could, he went downstairs.

In the drawing room, the lights were low.

Ross reclined, languidly almost, on the sofa.

Oscar paced, speaking quickly, exhibiting a high nervous energy, almost possessed.

'A university education is an admirable thing, of course. So long as you remember that nothing that is worth knowing can be taught. Least of all at Cambridge.'

'But you told me,' said Ross, 'in Greece, in ancient Greece, the older men taught the younger. They drew them out. I look forward to being drawn out immensely.'

'Well, Greek love – Platonic love – is the highest form of affection known to man, of course.'

'You also told me,' continued Ross, 'the Greeks put statues of Apollo in the bride's chamber, so she would have beautiful sons.'

Ross paused before delivering the *coup de grâce*.

'I can't help noticing that here the statue's in your bedroom.'

'Constance prefers a bath,' said Oscar hoarsely.

Ross laughed, then stood and walked boldly over. He stopped only inches away from Oscar, and stared deeply into his eyes.

Oscar sighed. He became aware of Constance's presence in the room above. 'She was so beautiful when I married her, Robbie.' He gazed within, down the long corridor of memory, and what he saw made him sad. 'Slim, white as a lily, such dancing eyes – I've never seen such love in a pair of eyes, she – she was – oh God!'

Ross reached up, caressed Oscar's cheek, then took his face in his hands and kissed him fully on the lips.

Oscar hesitated for a brief moment, but was incapable of holding back. He returned the kiss and was instantly lost in it.

It was Ross who broke the embrace and walked away. With his back to Oscar, he began to undress. He removed his shirt with despatch, then turned and faced Oscar again, squarely. He was unbuttoning his trousers and undergarments, moving more slowly now. Smiling openly, ingenuously, he responded to Oscar's anguish.

'Nothing should reveal the body but the body.'

Oscar's mouth was suddenly too dry to allow speech.

'Didn't you say?' said Ross. His trousers were loose about his hips as he moved toward Oscar once again.

'There has to be a first time for everything, Oscar. Even for you.'

Ross took Oscar's hands and placed them around his own slim waist. Then he gently pushed Oscar's hands down his hips, peeling away as he did so his last layer of garments.

Oscar took Robbie in his arms. This time there was no hesitation at all.

CHAPTER 4

The pulse of joy that beats in us at twenty, becomes sluggish. Our limbs fail, our senses rot. We degenerate into hideous puppets, haunted by the memory of the passions of which we were too much afraid, and the exquisite temptations that we had not the courage to yield to. Youth! Youth! There is absolutely nothing in the world but youth!

THE LATE AFTERNOON sunlight slanted into the nursery, revealing a scene of beatific domesticity. Constance was nursing Vyvyan, while the nanny was testing the water for Cyril's bath. Cyril was trying to escape the coming ordeal by any means possible, but mostly by screaming.

Oscar watched from a little distance, smoking a cigarette. He was dressed in evening clothes, and was both of the moment and entirely removed at the same time. It was not as if the people in the room were strangers to him, certainly not that. But their images, in the rich, mote-filled light, seemed to reach him through a kaleidoscopic filter of stained glass. Their voices, too, emanated from some great distance, but instead of becoming muted, they seemed to achieve an unusual clarity.

The nanny muttered an almost constant stream of scolding and reassurance.

'Now then, Cyril, you've got to get undressed. I know you hate it. Boys, Mrs Wilde! They never do what they're told!'

Constance paused in her nursing long enough to look up and notice Oscar. 'We're going to have a girl next time. Aren't we, Oscar?'

Oscar chose not to hear her. He kept his attention on Cyril. The effort of responding would have been too much.

'Mr Wilde had a sister who died, you see,' continued Constance. 'She was called Isola.'

'That's an unusual name,' said the Nanny.

'It means island, in Italian,' Oscar said. He did not look up, seeing for a moment the image of his sweet, lost sister superimposed on Cyril's equally sweet face. 'My mother has Italian blood.'

Constance smiled. 'She was thinking of the Emerald Isle, wasn't she?'

'Hard to know what's going on in my mother's mind. So much Celtic mist.' Oscar experienced his own kind of mist as well. He blinked, shattering the tiny prism of a tear.

Oscar glanced at his watch. 'I must go.'

He walked over to Constance to kiss her goodbye. As he approached her, there was no avoiding seeing his new son, Vyvyan, at his mother's breast.

He was at once repelled and intensely moved. As a model of self-involved maternity, Constance reminded him of nothing so much as a placid bovine animal, mindlessly content and hopelessly sentimental. Yet he desperately craved the nourishment and attention that she offered their child, and he longed for the physical intimacy they had shared in the past, however unsatisfying it had ultimately become. The melange of emotions that swept over him nearly knocked him over.

'Good night, my dear,' Oscar said. 'And you behave, Cyril. Remember, a gentleman should to take a bath at least once a year.'

He carefully contained himself, and, turning casually away, headed for the door.

'I shan't be back till late. I'm dining at the Asquiths'.'

Not at the Asquiths', but in a hotel room later that night, Oscar and Ross rested in bed. Their time together had brought comfort and joy, and their lovemaking was achieving a style and a pattern. Ross was usually the more active partner, and he would throw garments and bed-clothes every which way, baring himself to Oscar with the unconscious physical pride of the very young in love. In contrast to Ross's abandon, Oscar kept most of his clothes on, preferring a more diffident posture. Not only was he conscious of his size in relation to the diminutive Ross, but he was also painfully aware of being fifteen years the boy's senior.

Ross's eyes were closed, his head resting on Oscar's shoulder. Oscar kissed him on the lips, a quick, affectionate kiss. Ross opened his eyes and smiled.

'Do you love me?' he asked.

The question caught Oscar by surprise. Although his feelings for Ross were undeniable, and the boy was rarely out of Oscar's thoughts, he had somehow never had the matter posed quite that way. He felt a responsibility to respond seriously and accurately.

He took a moment to assemble his words, then began carefully and slowly, 'I feel like a city that's been under siege for twenty years, and suddenly the siege is lifted and the gates are thrown open, and all the citizens come pouring out . . .'

Ross giggled, as Oscar kept going.

'. . . to breathe the air, walk in the fields and pluck the wilde flowers – I feel *relieved*,'

Ross's giggles subsided, as he adjusted his position happily.

'You don't worry about Constance?'

Oscar thought about this for some time. Then he looked away, unable to answer.

CHAPTER 5

Art finds her own perfection within,
and not outside of, herself. She is not
to be judged by any external standards
of resemblance. She is a veil, rather
than a mirror. She has flowers that no
forests know of, birds that no woodland
possesses. She makes and unmakes many
worlds, and can draw the moon from
heaven with a scarlet thread. Hers are
the forms more real than living man,
and hers the great archetypes of which
things that have existence are but
unfinished copies. Nature has, in her
eyes, no law, no uniformity.

OVER THE NEXT three years, inspired at least in part by
Ross's companionship and wit, Oscar enjoyed a period
of heightened intellectual and creative activity. His essays
and stories were published everywhere, and his literary
works attracted more serious notice than before.

In *The Decay of Lying*, an essay written in the form of a
dialogue and derived directly from a conversation with

Ross, Oscar found the ideal forum for his contention that 'Life imitates Art far more than Art imitates Life'. Rather than mirroring life, he insisted, the artist had a profound responsibility to interpret, challenge, and ultimately transform the world around him.

Oscar's aesthetic not only reflected the double life he led, it encouraged and supported it. On the one hand, he wrote and published boisterous contemporary fiction like *Lord Arthur Savile's Crime*, expressing the quick and witty motion of his social life. On the other, he allowed a sadder and more stately tone to dominate his fairy tales. In these stories Oscar tackled the most difficult and painful subjects head on: cruelty, misery, suffering, disfigurement, good and evil, and, most particularly, the transfiguring power of love.

Although their presence was a gnawing reminder to Oscar of his deficiencies as a parent and a husband, his enthusiasm for his children was boundless, and the boys consumed his attention entirely when he was home. He would invent activities and games, and recite the tales of wonder he had invented to serve as new myths to live by, new models to emulate.

One afternoon in the nursery, Oscar was repairing damage to Cyril's fort, sticking together soldiers which had got broken. Cyril, now four, watched intently. Vyvyan, three years old, sat on Constance's knee.

As he worked, Oscar told them a story. The presence of the boys breathed life into it, and their questions and comments, mostly at this point Cyril's, endlessly encouraged him.

'Every afternoon, as they were coming home from school, the children used to play in the garden of the Selfish Giant.'

'Is that the garden where we go and play?' Cyril interrupted.

'No, this was much larger and lovelier than that, darling, with soft green grass and ...'

'There's green grass where we go.' This from Cyril again.

'Ah, but are there twelve peach-trees that burst into delicate blossoms of pink and pearl in the springtime, and bear rich fruit in the autumn?'

Cyril looked to Constance.

'Are there, Mama?'

'I don't think there are, Cyril, no.'

'No,' agreed Oscar. 'Hand me that matchstick, would you, and I'll put this hussar's head back on. Thank you.'

Cyril passed him the matchstick, and Oscar resumed his story.

'The birds sat on the trees and sang so sweetly that the children used to stop their games to listen. "How happy we are here!" they cried to each other.'

'I don't think they could be happy if there was a giant,' complained Cyril.

'Ah, but there wasn't. Not yet. He was away, visiting a friend.'

'You're always away,' commented Cyril seriously.

Oscar kept his head down, concentrating on the soldier he was mending, as he carefully constructed a response.

'Yes, but I only go away for a night or two at a time. And I always come back. Whereas this giant, the one whose garden it was, had been away for seven years. He was staying with an ogre in Cornwall, you see –'

'What's an ogre?'

'A sort of giant, but worse.'

Cyril was beginning to look distinctly scared.

Oscar changed his tone. 'And after seven years he'd said all he had to say, because his conversation was very limited.'

Constance laughed. Oscar looked up quickly, gave her a grateful smile, and then carried on.

'He decided to go back to his own castle. And when he arrived and found the children playing in his garden, he was very angry ...' Oscar put on a very gruff voice. ' "What are you doing here?" he cried. And all the children ran away. "My own garden is my own garden," said the Giant, "and I won't allow anyone to play in it except myself." So he built a high wall, all round, and put up a notice board on which was written in capital letters TRESPASSERS WILL BE PROSECUTED.

Here, Oscar was most appropriately interrupted by a knock on the door and the entrance of Arthur, the footman.

'Arthur, you're trespassing,' he said. 'Cyril will now eat you.'

'It's Mr Ross, sir, with Mr Gray,' announced Arthur.

Oscar abandoned the soldiers at once. It was as though a switch had been thrown. The boys were still there, and Constance, but Oscar was already elsewhere. He felt his speech quicken, his movements become hurried, as the momentum of his other life took him over.

'Good heavens, I must fly. The horses of Apollo are pawing impatiently at the gates.'

'I beg your pardon?' said the puzzled Cyril.

Oscar quickly pulled Cyril to him and kissed him. For a brief moment, his pace slowed. Robbie's world receded, as he looked into the boy's eyes and spoke.

'Papa must go.'

Then the tide was upon him again, and there was nothing he could do to stem its pull.

'You will come back and finish the story?' pleaded Cyril.

Oscar breathed a quick 'Of course I will'.

And he was gone.

A disappointed Cyril sat among his soldiers.

'Will he, Mama?' he asked.

'Of course he will, darling. Now, come on, Cyril, it's almost teatime!'

As the household returned to the efficiency that was customary in his absence, Oscar joined his companions in a cab downstairs.

After a year's stint at Cambridge, Ross's interests had turned to art and art criticism and he was contemplating running a gallery of his own. It became Oscar's pleasant duty to introduce Ross to the best and brightest – painters, critics, devotees and entrepreneurs – that London had to offer. Not so incidentally, these tours of the art world provided a perfect window for the socially curious, and a new frame for Oscar's expanding self-image. For many of those attending, such viewings were an opportunity to see and be seen, with the art often a mere backdrop for sly looks and whispered gossip.

This evening, for example, the private view of an exhibition of modern portraits was not necessarily the high point of the event. People were drinking and talking and not particularly looking at the pictures. They were looking, however, at Oscar, Ross and John Gray, a handsome young poet sporting a particularly aesthetic appearance, long hair flowing in waves to his shoulders and a Renaissance-style cap on top. The flamboyant trio strolled the gallery with an air of the elite.

Passing a painting of a beautiful young woman by a Pre-Raphaelite artist, Gray commented, 'I really don't know why people bother painting portraits any more. You can get a much better likeness with a photograph.'

Ross objected, 'Oh, but a photo's just one moment in time, one gesture, one turn of the head.'

'Yes, a portrait's not a likeness, Mr Gray,' explained Oscar. 'Painters show the soul of the subject, the essence.'

'The essence of the sitter's vanity, you mean,' said Gray.

They paused at another picture. 'Well,' whispered Ross, 'this is a portrait of Lady Battersby as a young woman. She's over there, as a matter of fact.' Gray glanced surreptitiously over his shoulder. 'I must go and console her,' concluded Ross.

There was no stopping him, once a target was in his sights. Ross hurried over to a wrinkled but pleasant old Lady Battersby, leaving Gray to look from the flesh to the portrait and back again, and to comment, 'Poor thing. I expect in her heart she thinks she still looks like this.' He sighed. 'If we could look young and innocent for ever ...'

Gray continued to gaze at the picture, much saddened, while Oscar looked at him, not saddened at all, and asked, 'Ah, but do you think we'd want to?'

'If our souls were ugly, yes.'

Oscar thought for a moment. An idea was catching hold.

'Give a man a mask, and he'll tell you the truth.'

'I like a face that tells the truth,' admonished Gray.

'Yours is truthful, as well as beautiful,' said Oscar. His eyes met Gray's. Gray held Oscar's look, seriously and without a flinch. Oscar found this very seriousness disarming. A quickening heartbeat tolled the young man's intellectual gifts as well as his even more obvious physical virtues.

'Have we had enough of this?' asked Oscar evenly. 'Shall we go and dine somewhere?'

Ross watched them go. As fond as he was of Oscar, he remained quite unsentimental about their relationship. Oscar had never professed undying love, and fidelity amongst their circle was neither expected nor usually wished for.

He smiled when he saw Oscar's arm go round Gray's shoulder, as the two left the gallery.

The evening on the town with Gray ended at a hotel, where, true to form, Oscar kept most of his clothes on, though Gray, slim and beautiful, did not.

An open bottle of champagne and two half-filled glasses graced a nearby table as Gray, aggressive and excited, kissed Oscar passionately. His manner was less sophisticated than Ross's, and much more direct.

'Please let me ... Oscar, please ... please let me ... please ...' he was whispering fiercely, while pulling at Oscar's clothing. Gently, tenderly, Oscar prevented him, manoeuvering to push Gray down on to the sofa.

'John, John, John. You are very young, and you are very beautiful.' Oscar kissed the lad and then gazed upon him. His eyes grew larger, as if to consume all that youth and beauty. They were nothing less than sustenance for his very soul.

Gray was put out and disappointed, but after a moment

he gracefully submitted, lying back. When they resumed their lovemaking, it was on Oscar's terms.

Oscar's behaviour was not without its effect on Constance. She knew, of course, that something was wrong, and she felt driven to look for solace and understanding in the most unexpected places.

On one occasion, she sought out Speranza, arriving at the Grosvenor Square house nearly breathless and in some considerable distress. As usual, the curtains were drawn, although it was the middle of the day, and she had to peer closely to see the full range of expressions on her mother-in-law's face.

Speranza was being ecstatic and most unhelpful. She waved about a small cigar she was smoking, and her very soul seemed to flutter in her fingers as she expounded on the state of Wildean art.

'*The Picture of Dorian Gray* is the most wonderful book I ever read. And the end, when the servants break in and find him wizened, old and dead, and the picture young again – I fainted!'

'My family say it's dull and wicked,' countered Constance.

'Dull?' Speranza laughed for some time at the sheer absurdity of the thought. 'It's sublime! It's about the masks we wear as faces, and the faces we wear as masks, it's … it's … that my son should have written a work of such supreme … Oscar is the greatest jewel that Irish literature has ever seen!'

'People say it's full of dangerous paradoxes. They don't seem to understand them,' said Constance.

'No, it's because they don't want to. Paradox is the only

way that we Irish can sometimes irritate the English into some semblance of rational thought. Connie, at last I feel my life is justified!'

Constance needed to be heard and, despite Speranza's barrage, she tried again, more directly, the catch of tears just under her voice.

'Hardly anyone will speak to us any more. We're ceasing to be respectable.'

Speranza stared at her, then reached out to take her hand. This was a token gesture to show that in some manner Speranza understood and sympathised. She continued lecturing, but in a softer tone.

'Artists care nothing about respectability. Oh, it's only jealousy! It's the spite of the untalented for the man of genius!'

Then she changed the subject. 'Where is Oscar?'

Constance pounced on the question. This was the opening for which she had been waiting. It seemed Speranza understood after all.

'He's in the Lake District. Writing a play, he says.'

'A drama?' Speranza was thrilled.

'A comedy.' That was hardly the point for Constance. 'Robbie Ross has gone to keep him company.' She paused, looking quizzically at her mother-in-law. Her tears were very close now. What could she possibly say? 'I do like Robbie.'

'And they both love you,' replied Speranza steadily. But then she lost herself once again in the rapture of her son's greatness, 'Oh, it'll be a success! Oscar is made for the stage!'

CHAPTER 6

*I love acting. It is so much more real
than life.*

O N 20 FEBRUARY 1892, *Lady Windermere's Fan* opened at
the St James's Theatre.

On the street outside, cabs and carriages lined up for the
end of the play, and horses and drivers both were startled
by the huge burst of applause for the final curtain. .

Backstage, Oscar watched from the wings nervously. He
wore a green carnation, and carried a lit cigarette in a
mauve-gloved hand. The actors moved back and forth,
jostling each other to take yet another bow. The curtain call
seemed endless, the applause loud and long, the curtain
going up, coming down, going up; rising and falling in a
motion that served only to make Oscar queasy. There were
louder and louder cries for the author.

Oscar prepared himself. He put on his customary mask of
total confidence and composure.

He sauntered on, and the applause redoubled.

He took centre stage, brandishing his cigarette, and with
a small gesture of his hand quieted the audience.

'Ladies and gentlemen, I have enjoyed this evening immensely.'

There was a burst of laughter.

'The actors have given us a charming rendering of a delightful play, and your appreciation has been most intelligent. I congratulate you on the great success of your performance, which persuades me that you think almost as highly of the play as I do myself.'

Throughout his speech, Oscar felt the laughter build with every phrase, until he bowed his exit to an even greater, more violent burst of applause.

The first-night party was held in the opulently decorated bar of the theatre, and it was an event of unparalleled flamboyance. Among those attending, besides the cast of the play, were dozens of young men wearing green carnations, a tribute to Oscar's penchant for artifice.

Constance and Ada were there, and Ross, of course, and John Gray, who greeted Oscar as he entered the bar.

'It went so well, Oscar, even better than I'd ...' He hesitated. 'They loved it, they absolutely loved it.'

'And I, dear boy, love you,' whispered Oscar, before being pulled away to greet the rest of the gathering.

Ada was first by his side, 'Oscar.'

'Sphinx,' he countered.

'You really must be careful. You are in grave danger of becoming rich.'

Ada was interrupted by Ross, who smiled a smile of genuine and unaffected congratulations.

'It was wonderful, as I knew it would be.'

'Thank you, Robbie.'

'Everyone's dying to know,' Ross continued, 'who the real Lady Windermere is.'

'The real Lady Windermere,' replied Oscar, 'is every woman in this room, and most of the men.'

Then Oscar was suddenly accosted by Lionel Johnson, a diminutive alcoholic poet, whom he remembered from a few previous social encounters.

'Oscar. Wonderful play,' Johnson said. 'My cousin, Lord Alfred Douglas, is here. He would very much like to congratulate you.'

Oscar knew Douglas, who was universally known as Bosie, to be the youngest son of the Marquess of Queensberry, a mixed blessing at best, but he was not aware that the young man was obsessed. The year before, Johnson had lent Bosie his copy of *The Picture of Dorian Gray*, and the book had a shattering effect on him. He responded instantly to the novel's key questions of image, role reversal and the relation of passion to art. He read it fourteen times running, and finally insisted on being introduced to the author. Johnson had immediately arranged for a visit to the Wildes'.

Oscar saw Bosie from across the room, and for a moment it was as if everyone else had ceased to exist.

Less shy than he had been at their first meeting, Bosie, now twenty-two, stared at Oscar with a volatile mixture of insolence and admiration. His head was cocked at a slight angle, and he was serious, so very serious. His features seemed to Oscar to have been chiselled out of the stone of antiquity, then turned by magic into living, breathing, softest flesh. He wore a tragic mien, as if he were an Orestes or a young Pentheus.

Oscar immediately found the force of Bosie's gaze,

augmented by his great beauty, quite dazzling and irresistible, as Johnson led him through the assemblage to Bosie's side.

'Oscar, this is Bosie Douglas.'

'We met last year, Lionel brought me to tea at Tite Street,' Bosie said. His voice had a richness and intensity about it that contrasted strangely with the cold accents of his class and struck a spark of fire in Oscar's breast.

'How could I forget?'

Bosie's manner was forthright to the point of arrogance. He was clearly not afraid at all.

'I love your play,' he said. 'The audience didn't know whether you meant your jokes or not. You shocked them – especially with your speech. But the more frivolous you seem, the more serious you are, aren't you? I love that.'

'Thank you,' replied Oscar, rising to the compliment. 'I always say, the young are the only critics with the experience to judge my work.'

'We need shocking,' continued Bosie, barely acknowledging the compliment. 'People are so banal. And you use your wit like a foil – you cut through all those starched shirt-fronts. You draw blood. It's magnificent. I wish you'd draw some blood at Oxford. Though you'd need a miracle. All the dons at my college have dust in their veins.'

Oscar laughed lightly. He was delighted, gratified and impressed by the young man's irreverence.

'Ah. At which college do you educate the fellows?'

'Magdalen,' said Bosie.

'My own college! Well, I shall claim the privilege of a graduate to come and take tutorials with you.'

'Come soon, then. They're threatening to send me down.'

'How could they be so cruel to one so beautiful?'

The pause that followed seemed to Oscar to last for a month.

When Bosie responded, his insignificant words were heavily loaded with the weight of what was unspoken. 'Dons . . . they're so middle class.'

This exchange and the ferocious magnetic attraction of the two men were not lost on others in the room, among them Gray, who looked on with anxiety. To his relief, it was at this point that the conversation was interrupted by the appearance of George Alexander, the actor-manager responsible for commissioning, encouraging and then producing the play. Alexander had rejected an earlier historical play, *The Duchess of Padua*, on the grounds that the scenery would be too expensive, and convinced Oscar to write on a modern subject instead.

'My dear Oscar,' boomed Alexander, 'you've shocked the whole of London, smoking on stage like that.'

With a look, Bosie made it clear to Oscar that he thought this comment pathetic, which in turn delighted Oscar no end.

'Excellent, then we shall run for a year!' Oscar quipped.

Under cover of Alexander's interruption, Gray managed to distract Oscar briefly away from Bosie.

'Oscar, you must say something to Marion Terry,' he said.'

Looking across the room, Oscar saw that the starring actress was entertaining admirers in regal splendour. Speaking as much to Bosie as to Gray, Oscar said, 'She was good, wasn't she? So good, in fact, I think she wrote most of the part herself.'

Bosie laughed and their eyes locked again.

'Excuse me, Lord Alfred,' said Oscar, reluctant to leave.

'Bosie – please.'

'Bosie,' agreed Oscar with a light bow, as he moved away, leaving Gray singularly unreassured.

Once *The Selfish Giant* was published, it became Constance's habit to read it to the children. They were now seven and six, and they never tired of hearing it.

'He was a very selfish giant. The poor children had nowhere to play. They tried to play on the road, but the road was dusty and full of hard stones, and they did not like it. They used to wander round the high walls of the Giant's garden when their lessons were over, and talk about the beautiful garden inside. "How happy we were there!" they said to each other.'

The parallels between Oscar and the giant were not lost on Constance, and she would often look up, wistful for a moment or two, before the boys would make her continue the reading.

It became Oscar's habit to walk with Bosie beside the river in Magdalen College garden. The romantic, nearly idyllic, setting contrasted sharply with the fierce landscape of Bosie's mind, where convoluted intrigues and expensive adventures were hatched hourly. Oscar found both worlds appealing, though, and the contrast kept him awake and alive.

One typical afternoon, as they strolled arm-in-arm, Bosie wore a jaunty straw hat, but his thoughts were on serious matters, and he so desperately wanted Oscar's help and approval.

'I hope he was a very *beautiful* boy?' Oscar said, when Bosie had finished his story.

'Well – pretty, you know, in a street Arab sort of way,' said Bosie, trying to sound sophisticated, but really quite insecure.

'There's no point in being blackmailed by an ugly one,' said Oscar.

'What's tiresome is, he's threatening to show my letters to my father.'

'Who will show them to all his friends, I'm sure, for the excellence of their style.'

Oscar's apparent flippancy was more than Bosie could stand, and his airs all abandoned him at once. Instantly, he transformed into little more than an unhappy child.

'No. No. You don't know him. He's a brute. Really. He carries a whip wherever he goes. He used to beat my mother, he beat my brothers, he thrashed me from the age ...' Bosie's voice trailed away, and he shivered.

Oscar, shocked, put an arm round him.

'My dear boy –'

Buoyed up by this show of affection from Oscar, Bosie recovered some of his bravado.

'Of course, he's practically illiterate, he probably won't understand the letters anyway.'

Oscar laughed.

'By an unforgivable oversight, I've never been black-mailed myself, but my friends assure me that a hundred pounds will usually suffice.'

'Really? God, I thought ...' Bosie breathed a sigh of relief. 'You promise?'

'Leave it to Lewis,' said Oscar. 'George Lewis, my lawyer. He knows what he's doing. He acts for the Prince of Wales.'

For Bosie, it was as though a cloud had passed, and he brightened visibly.

Bosie had a piano in his rooms at Magdalen and, later that day, he entertained Oscar and a small group of his college friends by singing for them. That afternoon, it was the lyrical duet from Gilbert and Sullivan's *The Pirates of Penzance*, which he sang solo and with a romantic intensity.

> *Oh, leave me not to pine,*
> *Alone and desolate.*
> *No fate seems fair as mine,*
> *No happiness so great.*

His friends were very impressed by Oscar's presence, and they sought to please him at every opportunity.

'Isn't he killing, Mr Wilde?' whispered one undergraduate, as Bosie sang on.

With complete sincerity, Oscar replied, 'He's perfect. He's perfect in every way,' as Bosie sang Mabel's lyrics rather than Frederick's, thereby switching the gender of the ending chorus, and finishing the roundelay with:

> *He loves me, he is here,*
> *Fa la la.*

The long silence that followed, in which Bosie and Oscar gazed at each other across the room with great intensity, was noted by the undergraduates present.

Not that Oscar cared. This was an enchanted world to him. He was surrounded by young men, music and the heady atmosphere of college youth.

Lying in a punt on the River Cherwell on late afternoons, he would look up at the lithe young Bosie, who, straw hat on head, sleeves rolled up, manoeuvered the punt-pole with grace and skill. To Oscar it felt as though these days would last for ever.

The nights too were filled with great tenderness. When Oscar looked at Bosie asleep on a divan, draped loosely in a sheet, limbs every which way, he saw a vision from the dim Platonic past he had so often extolled in his lectures and essays. This life was real, though, and he was living it with Bosie. Just out of the corner of his eye, Oscar could imagine another observer watching him and Bosie together, an observer who could not be otherwise than enchanted by the idyllic beauty before him. Their love existed in imitation of the greatest couples of antiquity, not pale, but vibrant with the colours of Oscar's immensely sensitive palette.

They were inseparable.

The world looked on. The world commented. The world nodded or shook its collective head, or applauded, or sneered or clicked its tongue. On occasion, the world intruded.

The lovers paid it little mind.

In a hotel restaurant in Oxford, a head waiter tried to seat the two men off in a corner of the dining room.

Bosie complained. 'I don't want to sit here. I want to sit there.' He pointed to a table in the centre of the room. 'I want everyone to look at us.'

The waiter looked at Oscar dubiously.

'You heard what Lord Alfred said.'

With a bow and a flourish, they were shown to the

centre table. As they sat, Bosie spoke very clearly, as if for all to hear.

'I want people to say, Look, there's Oscar Wilde with his boy.'

Oscar beamed with delight at this deliberate provocation. He was in love with Bosie, yes, but also with his daring. It had all seemed too safe before. His time with Ross and Gray had, in retrospect, a security about it that Oscar was now anxious to shed. If his life, this aesthetic edifice that he had so painstakingly raised, was to have a purpose, it needed to be seen and allowed to have its effect upon the world.

Two waiters produced menus and spread their napkins for them as though they hadn't heard a word.

'So, what shall we let people see us eating?' asked Oscar. The game was a fine one indeed.

'Foie gras and lobster,' said Bosie. 'And champagne.'

Oscar closed the menu and smiled at the waiter.

'For two. We do everything together.'

'Very good, Mr Wilde,' said the waiter, moving off to see to their order.

Bosie lit a cigarette, and then, as if challenging the other diners to do something about it, he reached slowly across the table, and placed the cigarette delicately and sensuously between Oscar's lips.

By now people were beginning to look. And they looked all afternoon at this outrageous couple. They listened as well, though none there would admit it openly, to the brash and wickedly witty conversation.

Oscar and Bosie outlasted their audience, though, and in time the restaurant became empty, save for them, an oasis of sparkle and warmth in a darkening afternoon desert of long shadows and abandoning tables. Their only accompaniment was the whispering of a few waiters conferring in corners.

'All my family are mad,' Bosie confessed. He was concluding a diatribe on a subject which he found both frustrating and colourful. 'My uncle slit his throat last year. In a railway hotel.'

'Which station?'

'Euston.'

'Ah, all life's most serious journeys involve a railway terminus.' Oscar looked at his watch. 'And now I must go to the station myself.'

He smiled lovingly at Bosie. 'Sarah Bernhardt thinks she knows better than I do how to play Salomé.'

The formidable actress, whom Oscar had called 'that serpent of Old Nile', was indeed in rehearsal for the title role in his French play. They would discuss costume and style interminably.

'Stay,' said Bosie. 'Please stay. At least till this evening.'

Oscar hesitated only a moment.

'Sarah is divine as you are. She will be wonderful at the play's climax, when Salomé kisses the lips of the severed head of John the Baptist.'

With this Oscar began to act out the scene to an enthralled Bosie. ' "Ah, thou wouldst not suffer me to kiss thy mouth, Jokanaan." Jokanaan is the old Hebrew name for John. "Well! I will kiss it now. I will bite it with my teeth as one bites a ripe fruit. Yes, I will kiss thy mouth, Jokanaan. Thy body is white like the snows that lie on the mountains of Judaea, and come down into the valleys ..." '

They were soon inflamed by the lines. For Oscar, speaking his own delicious words to Bosie was like biting into a ripe fruit. It was intoxicating in a special way, all faculties — senses, intellect and imagination — working together at a feverish pitch. For Bosie it was his wildest dream and greatest ambition come true.

There was no stopping them. They repaired to Bosie's room, where they made mad and passionate love.

Considerably later, Bosie stood naked, smoking a cigarette. He was turned away from Oscar, in a sort of teasing shyness, his body striking an easy relaxed pose more than reminiscent of Michelangelo's *David*.

Oscar gazed upon him and gently, softly, completed the recitation.

' "The roses in the garden of the Queen of Arabia are not so white as thy body." '

Bosie turned and caught Oscar's eye. He smiled, still somehow shy, this boy.

And loving.

Oscar never doubted his love.

CHAPTER 7

*A great poet, a really great poet, is the
most unpoetical of creatures. But
inferior poets are absolutely fascinating.
The worse their rhymes the more
picturesque they look. The mere fact of
having published a book of second-rate
sonnets makes a man quite irresistible.
He lives the poetry he cannot write.
The others write the poetry that they
dare not realize.*

LADY MOUNT-TEMPLE HAD a house at Babbacombe Cliff,
near Torquay in Devon. It was an extravagant Pre-
Raphaelite showplace designed by John Ruskin, one of
Oscar's early idols. All the rooms had names. The bedrooms
bore the names of the flowers featured in the wallpaper,
and Georgina's own boudoir, called simply Wonderland,
was hung with paintings by Rossetti and Burne-Jones.

Over the years, Lady Mount-Temple had taken Constance, who was in some baroque fashion a distant cousin,
under her wing. Although she sat in judgement on the rest
of the world, she was singularly tolerant of Constance and

her sons. Constance enjoyed visiting, for indeed only here could she feel at peace and fully taken care of. She would take the boys to Babbacombe Beach, where Cyril and Vyvyan would play enthusiastically in the sand, supervised by their nanny, leaving her to gaze quietly out at the ocean. There she could sometimes catch glimpses of the map of her past, while casting about for clues as to her future.

Georgina was a welcome and not infrequent companion, and they would talk with the utter candour of lonely women.

One blustery day, they sat in beach chairs in the shelter of the sea-wall, straw hats carefully anchored, the white cliffs stunningly bright in the sunshine. Constance lay back almost languidly, as if her whole body were a pout, reporting on Oscar's more public activities, specifically the newest scandal surrounding *Salome*.

'Oscar's furious,' she said.

'He has no right to be,' lectured Lady Mount-Temple, upright in her chair as in her convictions. 'He knew perfectly well that the Lord Chamberlain would never allow a play with biblical characters. He never has done.'

'Oscar doesn't think there should be censorship of plays at all.'

'Of course there must be censorship. Or people would say what they meant, and then where should we be? When is he coming to join us?'

'He's not,' said Constance wistfully. 'He must stay and look after Lord Alfred.'

'Aughh! Those Douglases are always ill. When they're not demented. One of them, you know, he roasted a kitchen-boy on a spit.'

Constance looked up in alarm. Horrified, she encouraged Georgina to continue.

'And Bosie's father – Lord Queensberry – oh, he's a dreadful man, Constance. Doesn't believe in God. Or marriage. He bullies his wife into divorcing him; then he won't pay what the lawyers agree. It's disgraceful.' She paused, and looked out to sea with a faint smile, remembering someone raffish from her otherwise highly respectable past. 'I don't know what it is about sporting men, they just don't seem able to contain themselves.' Sweeping her memory aside, she returned to the present and the subject at hand. 'A Marquess should set a proper example. Or what are the upper classes for? I tell you, I wouldn't want any daughter of mine to marry a Douglas.'

There was a long silence. Then Constance said, 'I haven't got a daughter.' There was a sharpness in her comment that Georgina chose to ignore.

'If he'd gone to Canada, say, or Australia, Queensberry might have turned out all right. But . . .' Beginning to warm once again to her subject, Georgina was stopped cold by the sight of Constance looking sadly out to sea. She clucked lightly, then consoled her as brightly as she could, 'Plenty of time still, my dear.'

Constance shook her head, just once, wryly. To which Georgina could only respond with, 'Oh. Oh, I see!'

Embarrassed, but determined to have her say, to let it all out, Constance continued, 'It's – it's my fault. After Vyvyan was born, all I could think of was the children.'

'Ah,' Georgina sighed. There was another long silence, as they both continued to stare out at the sea. 'So that's why Oscar spends so much time with his men friends.'

'Men do like to be with one another, don't they?'
Constance looked to Georgina for reassurance.

'Some men, yes. Men of an age. Not usually men of
Oscar's age or …' Georgina caught a look of such pitiable
vulnerability on Constance's face that it caused her to
stumble, '… or Bosie's.' She paused before continuing,
dryly, 'Sometimes I think there ought to be a law against
men.'

Constance managed a smile. She marshalled her loyalty.

'Oscar needs disciples. And Lord Alfred's a poet, a very
fine poet, Oscar says.'

Georgina could only look doubtful.

'He's studying classics,' Constance said. 'Oscar and he,
they talk about Plato and so on.'

Georgina raised her eyebrows. Constance suddenly felt
rattled, and sought the older woman's assurance yet again:
'There's nothing wrong, really there isn't.'

'It's not whether there's anything wrong,' Lady Mount-
Temple invoked with quiet authority. 'It's whether or not
there appears to be. That's all people care about. The empire
was not built by men like Bosie Douglas.'

The Cheshire Cheese Pub off Fleet Street had been a
traditional gathering place for gentlemen of literary pursuits
for centuries. So it was not uncommon to find Oscar and
Bosie there, along with an expanding set of admiring young
men. One particular evening, in addition to Ross and an
increasingly unhappy John Gray, Oscar's table boasted
Gray's cousin Lionel Johnson and Ernest Dowson. Both
were serious and accomplished poets, self-consciously
decadent. Both were on their way to an early death – thanks
to excessive drinking.

Even among such illustrious company, it was always Bosie who sat on Oscar's right hand, and this night it was Bosie who held forth with a poem of his own.

'– *And the bay lay still,*
In a dream.
And the hours forgot to pass.
And you came, my love, so stealthily,
That I saw you not,
Till I felt that your arms were hot
Round my neck, and my lips were wet
With your lips, I had forgot
How sweet you were. And lo! the sun has set
And the pale moon came up silently.'

The end of the poem was greeted with another kind of silence. Johnson caught Dowson's eye, and spoke to him *sotto voce.* 'I've never heard a noisy moon? Have you?'

Dowson almost choked, hiding quickly in his drink to smother both his laughter and his dismay at the quality of the writing.

From his throne some seats away, Oscar intoned, 'I don't know which is more beautiful, Bosie or his poem.'

'Why doesn't someone else read a poem?' suggested Johnson quickly. 'John?' Gray shook his head, angrily. He was too jealous and furious to speak. Johnson turned to Dowson. 'Ernest – you've got something, I'm sure.'

'Nothing new,' Dowson mumbled, still trying to keep his laughter under control.

But Johnson, terrified that Bosie might begin yet another recitation, would not accept no for an answer, 'Give us one of your old ones, then,' he persisted, adding in a whisper, 'Let's have a poem for God's sake!'

This comment was, alas, loud enough to be heard by all, and it provoked an awkward exchange of looks among the group. Bosie, insulted, looked to Oscar for appropriate redress. Oscar, for a moment unsure of his footing, looked at Ross, who shrugged.

'Yes, tell us again about Cynara, Ernest,' encouraged Oscar at last, recalling Dowson's best-known work. 'Tell us how you've always been faithful to Cynara.'

Dowson made an effort, pulled himself together, and started his poem.

> 'Last night, ah, yesternight, betwixt her lips and mine
> There fell thy shadow, Cynara! thy breath was shed
> Upon my soul between the kisses and the wine,
> And I was desolate and sick of an older passion.
> Yea, I was desolate, and bowed my head.
> I have been faithful to thee, Cynara! in my fashion.
> All night upon mine heart, I felt her warm heart beat,
> Night long, within mine arms, in love and sleep she lay.
> Surely, the kisses of her bored, red mouth were sweet ...'

As Dowson continued, passionately and very much from the heart, much of the tension in the room was released.

Only Bosie and Gray maintained a sullen hurt ferocity, feeding on Dowson's words.

Able to endure it no longer, Gray got up and went to the bar. After a moment, Ross followed. As he approached, Gray gulped down one drink and quickly ordered another.

Sensing Ross's arrival, Gray did not bother looking up. He began to speak, from the soul, as if to his drink, 'I'm not good enough for him any more,' he said. 'I'm just the son of a carpenter, while Bosie —'

'Oscar's only ever been smitten before,' explained Ross, trying to soothe him, 'He was smitten with me, he was smitten with you.'

'I wasn't smitten.' Gray insisted. He looked up and around. He paused, waiting for the bartender to move off. 'I loved him.'

'Well – now he's fallen in love,' Ross said gently.

'He makes everything seem so wonderful, purple and gold,' Gray continued wretchedly. 'And when – when he casts you aside for some titled ...' Gray began to shake. 'I'm halfway to hell-fire. I'm not joking.'

'Someone else was a carpenter's son,' reminded Ross, with genuine sympathy, eliciting a startled stare from Gray. 'I've given in and become a Catholic,' said Ross. 'The Romans are so sensible about human frailty. Not like the Protestants, making you feel guilty all the time.' He paused for a moment. 'I find confession wonderfully consoling.'

'I can't go to confession when I – I want to kill Bosie. Or myself.'

Ross thought for a moment. 'Possessiveness is a sin. In Oscar's Church, at any rate. And mine, actually. I was his first, remember.'

At this point, Dowson's performance, reaching its pinnacle of passion, intruded upon their confessions.

> '... But I was desolate and sick of an old passion,
>   When I awoke, and found the dawn was grey.
>   I have been faithful to thee, Cynara! in my fashion.
>   I cried for madder music, and for stronger wine.
>   But when the feast is finished, and the lamps expire,

Then falls thy shadow, Cynara! the night is thine.
And I am desolate and sick of an old passion,
Yea, hungry for the lips of my desire:
I have been faithful to thee, Cynara! in my fashion.'

Ross and Gray returned to the group and the light patter of appreciative applause.

Oscar glanced in their direction, and smiled at them. That smile was so unaffectedly genuine that Gray's heart melted to see it.

CHAPTER 8

Then the Spring came, and all over the
country there were little blossoms and
little birds. Only in the garden of the
Selfish Giant it was still winter. The
birds did not care to sing in it as
there were no children, and the trees
forgot to blossom.

The Snow covered up the grass with
her great white cloak, and the Frost
painted all the trees silver. Then they
invited the North Wind to stay with
them, and he came. He was wrapped
in furs, and he roared all day about
the garden, and blew the chimneypots
down.

CYRIL AND VYVYAN stood at the nursery window, looking
out through the bars for their absent father, as the story
he had told them, now read to them mostly by their
mother, lost the cadence of their father's voice.

In the intimate world of London society, very little could
remain private and hidden. Against the most elaborate

efforts at secrecy, chance encounters and bizarre juxta-positions ruled.

For example, what if Constance were to enter the Savoy Hotel, as she might, passing Alfred Wood on his way out.

Neither would know the other, but the porter who held the door knew both, and would put two and two together. And a porter's discretion was not always guaranteed.

Upstairs at the Savoy hotel, Oscar and Bosie were having breakfast served in their sitting-room. Bosie was informal, in his dressing-gown, while Oscar was attired for the day.

They spoke of Oscar's latest play, *A Woman of No Importance*, which he had written under commission for Herbert Beerbohm Tree, an old friend who was now the manager of the Haymarket Theatre. Very impressed by *Lady Windermere's Fan*, Tree had been after Oscar to write a play for his theatre with a good role for him in it. Bosie had suffered a severe illness during the writing of the play, through which Oscar had nursed him, spending consequently even less time than usual with Constance and the boys. Perhaps the play too had suffered, but Oscar finished it nonetheless, and it was now into rehearsal, with Tree playing Lord Illingworth in a manner that vexed Oscar as being too overblown and theatrical.

Bosie tried to console Oscar, 'There's nothing to worry about. The play will get terrible notices and run for months. Oscar, it's wonderful.'

'Do you really think so?' asked Oscar, naively pleased with any praise from Bosie.

They heard a knock. The servant went to answer it.

'That's probably Tree now,' said Oscar, getting up and going to the door.

But it was Constance who appeared on the threshold. She seemed reticent and unsure of herself, but the power of her presence in this setting hit Oscar like a slap.

Momentarily dismayed, he recovered quickly, saying, 'My dear! How nice!' and kissing her on the cheek.

Bosie rose, all confidence, and was instantly at Oscar's side. 'Constance!' He too kissed her, like an old friend.

'Bosie ...' she said, and then stopped. All her resolution had abandoned her, and she had absolutely no idea what to say. Neither did anyone else. Turning back to Oscar, Constance regained just enough of her composure to rummage through her bag. 'I've brought your letters. You haven't been home for so long –'

With a quick 'Thank you' Oscar accepted the proffered post, and returned to the breakfast table.

'It's so much more convenient for Oscar, living in the West End, when he has a play coming on,' said Bosie.

'Yes, I'm like one of those northern businessmen keeping an eye on my factory,' Oscar agreed.

His comment was not received very well.

Oscar looked at the envelopes and, in his embarrassment, tried to be funny.

'Tite Street – Tite Street? Isn't that in Chelsea somewhere?'

This too fell very flat. Bosie, seeing that Constance was almost in tears, remained silent.

'The boys ask for you all the time. They're longing too see you,' she said finally, shaming Oscar.

'Oscar has to make sure the play's a success, Constance,' Bosie responded.

Oscar ignored Bosie. He panicked. There had to be a way

to make it right. For a moment he could not think at all. Then the idea came to him. Of course. It would be all right.

'I'll come this afternoon,' said Oscar quickly. 'For tea.'

'Oh, would you? They do miss you so much.'

'It's the dress rehearsal this afternoon,' Bosie reminded Oscar, almost under his breath.

Constance did not show her surprise, but simply waited, watching Oscar.

He looked down, aware of his patent weakness. He took a breath, with difficulty.

'Tomorrow, then. I'll come tomorrow. Yes, of course ...' Oscar's voice trailed away into nothingness.

'Tomorrow then,' said Constance, trying to sound casual. She walked over to Oscar, stooped over him, and kissed him gently on the forehead.

'Goodbye, my dear,' he said.

She hestitated only a moment before leaving. 'Goodbye,' she said sweetly. Then she turned and, in a rustle of skirts, was gone.

Bosie sprang eagerly to open the door for her. The look on his face as Constance left was one of triumph.

Full of guilt, Oscar tried to rationalise his feelings.

'She's so meek and forbearing! She's so *good*, I can't bear it!'

But saying these things did not make him feel any better. Although he did, of course, have other responsibilities he could not neglect.

One of Oscar's duties soon after was a visit to Lady Queensberry's house in Salisbury, a Victorian baronial gothic affair. He had been summoned.

Oscar looked up at the house nervously as he alighted

from his cab, very much like someone about to meet his mother-in-law for the first time. As he paid his fare and approached, Sybil Montgomery, the Marchioness of Queensberry and Bosie's mother, watched carefully from an upstairs window. Divorced from the Marquess of Queensberry five years earlier, she was devoted to Bosie, her youngest son, and much concerned about his shaky performance at Oxford. She had a suffering look, like someone who had just been struck and was still quivering from the blow. Beside her stood Lady Mount-Temple, whose social rounds had brought her, perhaps not coincidentally, to this particular crossroads.

'He doesn't look like a great wit,' said Lady Queensberry.

'My dear Sybil,' retorted her friend as Oscar's knock was heard, 'how can you tell with the Irish?'

In the drawing room, they sat close together, placing Oscar below them and at a disadvantage. They appeared to him as a pair of judges.

Lady Queensberry began the interrogation.

'If one is going to Oxford, Mr Wilde, one should, don't you think, do a little work? Or they send one down, and that's such a waste of time.'

'I don't know why you sent Bosie to Oxford in the first place,' said Lady Mount-Temple. 'All the Douglases are quite ineducable.'

Georgina never addressed Oscar directly, deferring to Lady Queensberry as the senior examiner.

'I was always in trouble at Oxford myself, Lady Queensberry,' pacified Oscar. 'But I still got a first.'

'You wouldn't want Bosie getting a first,' said Lady

Mount-Temple. 'That would be very morbid and middle-class.'

Before Oscar was able to formulate a reply, Lady Queensberry took her turn.

'He's been sent down once already.'

'I was rusticated, too,' he said.

'Well, that's just it,' she countered, 'He seems to be following all too literally in your footsteps.

'When he's not arm-in-arm with him,' interjected Lady Mount-Temple.

'All this poetry writing,' began Bosie's mother with a vague wave of disapproval.

'Bosie is a very brilliant young poet,' stated Oscar.

'Well, you say so, and he believes you,' she said. 'You're a very great influence on him. Everyone can see that.'

'Especially at the Café Royal and the Savoy,' added Lady Mount-Temple.

'You shouldn't encourage him to think so well of himself,' said Lady Queensberry. 'Bosie is very vain. We have always had to make a point of not praising Bosie.' She paused, as if momentarily distracted. 'And he's so *extravagant*. I don't know who he thinks is going to pay his debts. And now the President of Magdalen says it's more than likely he will fail his exams again.'

'It's the distractions,' insisted Lady Mount-Temple. 'All the distractions. London.'

It took Oscar a moment, still trying to make his way through this unexpected morass of questions, to realise that Georgina was, in fact, referring to him as the 'distractions'.

'I do urge him to study, Lady Queensberry,' he insisted with some firmness, rising to the challenge.

'Yes, well …' She thought about this. 'The President tells

me Bosie has improved of late. He appears to be benefiting from your company in that way, at least.'

Oscar raised an eyebrow in surprise, as did Lady Mount-Temple. Lady Queensberry turned to her.

'He says Mr Wilde's relationship with Bosie is very Greek, Georgina. He says he draws him out.'

Oscar, speechless for once, could only sputter, 'Well ... well I –'

'And, of course, his father is useless.'

'Certifiable,' agreed Lady Mount-Temple.

'I rely on you, Mr Wilde. Bosie is to work. No more of this lunching in London. I want you to draw Bosie out so he passes this wretched exam.'

And with that, the interview was concluded.

Oscar descended the steps of the house in a mild state of shock tempered with fine amusement. His duty had certainly been clearly laid out. But what did the Marchioness and her concerns have to do with him and with Bosie? Altogether nothing, he concluded, as he climbed into the waiting cab. After all, she surely did not know her son the way he did. She was, in her own way, as hopelessly out of touch with Bosie and his generation as Lord Queensberry himself.

Not surprisingly, whatever the deleterious effects on Bosie's academic career, he and Oscar continued to haunt London, and the Savoy Hotel in particular. The distractions of the city were real enough and, as the first bloom wore off their love, Oscar and his companion found that they responded quite differently to the charms London had to offer.

This was brought home one particular evening.

Bosie was lounging on the sofa in the sitting room, feet

up, reading a book and looking very beautiful. He was in shirt and vest.

Oscar came in from the bedroom and leaned against the door. He looked at Bosie longingly. Bosie, not in the mood, chose to ignore him.

Oscar, not to be put off, walked to the sofa and sat awkwardly by him. He caressed Bosie's neck in a way that had elicited a more positive response before. Without moving aside, looking up, or even acknowledging Oscar, Bosie unfastened a couple of shirt buttons. Then, still apparently intent on his book, he took Oscar's hand and placed it inside the shirt. It was as if he were granting Oscar the favour of entering some inner sanctum and fondling him.

After a few moments of this, Bosie finally raised his head and gave Oscar a searching look. He relented, closed his book and reached up to Oscar.

They met in a long, deep kiss.

Then, as if suddenly remembering a previous engagement, Bosie pulled back, rose abruptly, and began buttoning his shirt. He walked quickly away from Oscar, and approached a mirror.

Bosie looked at himself in the mirror, taking his measure. Then he turned back to Oscar. 'Let's go out,' he said, his brief words replete with boredom, impatience and a fierce longing to taste the pleasures of the London evening.

'If you like,' replied Oscar.

They were soon in a cab. Oscar pretended to be more cheerful than he felt. Bosie smirked, and played at being more knowing about something than Oscar. For once it was he who was the acknowledged expert on a subject, and he held forth enthusiastically.

'The thing about renters is, you don't have to consider their feelings,' he said.

'Oh, but if someone is willing to give one pleasure, one must feel gratitude at least.'

'No. Money, that's all they want. What's wonderful about going to Taylor's is, no one pretends. You just do it and be done with it.' He looked seriously at Oscar. 'I do love you, Oscar – but variety is the spice of life.'

Then Bosie took his hand and bestowed a lascivious smile on him, saying, 'You can watch me, if you like.'

He was being so wordly, so adult, that Oscar was actually enchanted. He sighed, and put a brave face on it.

'Let's feast with panthers, then!'

They arrived at the flat in Westminster to find that Alfred Taylor was a young man intent on going through a fortune as quickly as he could. To this end, he enlisted the services of other, even younger men, three of whom were present on this occasion. They were all consuming copious amounts of food and drink.

Bosie offered introductions all around in a genially convivial tone.

'Alfred Taylor, this is Oscar.'

'Delighted to make your acquaitance,' said Taylor with a smirk.

'There's Charlie Parker – I remember you.' Bosie pointed to a lad sitting on the arm of Taylor's chair. 'William Allen and Alfred Wood.'

Wood sat grinning on a sofa opposite. He seemed to know he had a very special victim in his sights.

'Hello, Oscar,' he said with great familiarity.

Oscar opened his case and offered the boy one of his elaborately tipped cigarettes. 'Do you smoke?'

'I do everything.'

Laughter and comment burst from around the room. 'Everything that pays ...' and 'Expertly, I might add ...'

Oscar took out a cigarette, lit it, then handed it to Wood, who gave a mock bow.

'Thank you! Nice case!'

Oscar nonchalantly handed it to him.

'I want you to keep it,' he said, looking around. There was something appealing to him about the casualness of the setting, the ease with which the young men took him into their world, and the patent acceptance of a way of life that was anathema to society at large. Even the danger – and he did feel at risk, from this nearly feral pack of youths, as well as from the simple fact of being with them – was distinctly seductive. Oscar felt powerful. He decided that in this jungle he could easily become the hunter.

'So this is a den of vice,' he commented. 'I should call it more of a garden. Such pretty flowers, Mr Taylor. How wise of you to keep the curtains closed. They would never grow in the common light of day.'

'Here, who are you calling common?' challenged Taylor, sensing an insult.

'Certainly not you, dear boy. You seem a flower of the rarest hue.'

During this exchange, Bosie crooked a finger at Wood, calling him over and thus instigating a complicated bit of matchmaking choreography. In seconds, Wood had walked across the room and sat in Bosie's lap, while Parker left Taylor's side to join Oscar.

Oscar lit another cigarette. 'Bosie never told me you were a botanist, Mr Taylor. That you roam the earth, climbing the highest peaks of the Himalayas, and plunging into the darkest forests of Borneo, to return triumphant to this delightful conservatory in the shadow of Westminster Abbey, to exhibit your specimens.'

Not quite sure how to respond to this barrage of elevated imagery, Taylor settled for, 'The boys are all Londoners, actually.'

'Impossible. I see Londoners every day, but never such exotic blooms as these.'

Wood and Bosie were on their feet now, moving together in a manner that was more provocative than graceful.

'Does he always talk like this?' lisped Wood.

Bosie laughed. 'Not when he's in bed.' As an illustration, he offered a gesture suggestive of Oscar with his mouth full.

Wood laughed, then the other boys.

Oscar sensed something a little sad in all this, but he smiled, almost too enthralled with his new power to care, as sweet young Charlie Parker nuzzled him.

In 1893 Bosie took a fancy to a house at Goring-on-Thames, and persuaded Oscar to rent it. In typical contradictory fashion, Oscar called it 'a most unhealthy and delightful place', and found 'The Cottage', as it was called, conducive for a time to romance, write and receive visitors.

Among his most cherished visitors were his family.

On a rare and lovely summer day, Oscar was with Cyril and Vyvyan. Carrying a variety of fishing paraphernalia, they walked jauntily across the river by means of a small footbridge and, on the other side, they found a small jetty under willow branches. There, with their feet cooling in the swirling water, the boys played at catching minnows with their little nets.

Oscar once again regaled them with The Selfish Giant, and the gently rushing river played a natural counterpoint to the tale, which the boys now knew by heart, loving it all the more for that, and for their father's telling of it.

' "I believe the Spring has come at last," said the Giant; and he jumped out of bed and looked out.'

The boys joined in, speaking together.

'And what did he see?' they shouted.

'Well? What did he see?' teased Oscar.

'You tell it,' said Cyril.

Oscar just then caught sight of Constance, walking towards them and waving.

'He saw a most wonderful sight,' he said.

Vyvyan yelled, 'Mama, mama!'

But Cyril was not to be distracted, 'No. Through a little hole ... You tell it, Papa.'

'Through a little hole in the wall the children had crept in,' Oscar continued, 'and they were sitting in the branches of the trees. In every tree that he could see there was a little child. And the trees were so glad to have the children back again that –'

And here again, Cyril, reaching one of their favourite parts, joined in, 'They'd covered themselves with blossoms –'

Vyvyan, not to be outdone, called out, 'Blossoms!' and then continued the story on his own. '– and were waving their arms gently above the children's heads. The birds were twittering and singing above them with delight, and the flowers were looking up through the green grass and laughing.'

'Oscar! Oscar!' Constance called out to them. She approached, nearly breathless, as her family rose from the bank to greet her. 'It's time the boys changed. We'll miss the train!'

'Oh, Papa, can't we stay?' cried out Cyril.

'Papa's got to work,' his mother called back. 'He's got to finish his play.'

Grimacing to himself, Oscar mumbled, 'Oh dear. Yes. Poor Papa!'

As the quartet walked back to the house, Cyril echoed the sound of his father's voice like a miniature brass band, chanting 'Poor, poor Papa . . . poor, poor Papa!' in a slow marching rhythm.

The house at Goring-on-Thames was not a cottage at all, but a magnificent mansion with lawns running down to the river. It was maintained lavishly, with eight servants and all the boats and sporting accoutrements that made for an ideal country house. Bosie had his own variety of guests in mind as well, and they visited in droves.

In his study, Oscar would sit at his desk writing. The sounds of lawn sports came in through the open window. Oscar had only to look up to see a group of Bosie's Oxford friends playing badminton and drinking champagne between shots.

Bosie, to keep fit, exercised his upper body by swinging a couple of weights in rhythm to the conversation.

'Where is Oscar?' asked one of his friends. 'We haven't seen him at all.'

'Where do you think he is?' responded Bosie. 'He's working. He is a writer after all.'

'I hear your father's threatening to shoot Lord Rosebery,' offered another friend after a short pause.

'Really? He usually favours the horsewhip,' said Bosie cheerfully.

'Says he's buggering your brother.'

'Well – Rosebery is Secretary of State for Foreign Affairs. And Francis is his private secretary.' There was laughter at this. 'But actually Francis is about to get engaged.'

'What's your father talking about, then?'

'Oh, he's obsessed with sex. He thinks Oscar's buggering me. As though I'd allow anyone to do that.'

Perhaps his friends were not convinced. Bosie did not get the kind of response he wanted, so, after a moment, he grinned a crooked grin, and added, 'I'm a bowler, not a batsman.' At least this comment elicited a laugh or two from the group.

Oscar was still at his desk, working on the first act of *An Ideal Husband*, when Bosie appeared, leaning in the doorway, bored and spoiling for a fight.

'I'm sick of the country,' he said.

There was no response from Oscar.

'Let's get back to London.'

Another pause.

'Well, what's the point of us living together if you're always working?'

Bosie entered the room and sat down on the edge of a divan, staring intently at Oscar, willing him to answer.

'I have responsibilities,' responded Oscar finally, 'a wife and family.'

'Oh, God, not that again! I ask my friends over from Oxford, and you just disappear!' Oscar raised his head, but suppressed the response that half-formed on his lips.

Gratified that he'd got some reaction out of Oscar, Bosie continued, 'I'd be better off staying at my mother's,' he reclined on the divan, no longer looking at Oscar, and casually tossed off, 'at least she's there.'

'Bosie, you asked me specifically to take this house so that we –'

'Well, now I'm bored with it! And with you!'

'I can't just give it up. It's paid for in advance. And until I finish my new play ...'

Bosie sniffed.

'Bosie, dear,' Oscar took a deep breath. He turned slowly toward Bosie, and, trying to combine reason with flattery, he began anew, 'You have beauty, you have breeding, and, most glorious of all, you have youth. But you are very fantastical if you think that pleasures don't have to be earned and paid for.'

'Whenever I want to do anything, you say you can't afford it. But you give all those renters cigarette cases.'

Oscar was flabbergasted. He felt his generosity had been boundless.

'But I've lavished presents on you,' he blurted. 'Every penny I've earned from my plays I have spent on you!'

'Oh, I'm sure you've been counting!' sneered Bosie, knowing full well that the accusation was outrageous, and not caring a jot. 'You're so mean and penny-pinching and middle-class, all you can think about is your bank balance.'

'Bosie, for God's sake, this is intolerable!'

'No gentleman ever has the slightest idea what his bank balance is!' shouted Bosie, offering Oscar a bit of his own back. 'You're absurd! Telling everyone how they ought to live – you're so vulgar – I never want to see you again! Ever!'

'All right!' cried Oscar. 'If that's what you want, then … Go! Go! Get out! Go!'

Bosie stormed out.

Through the window, Oscar could see the empty canoe tied up by the river bank and, as tears began to form, the words that came to him were from *The Selfish Giant*. He could just picture his son, Cyril, almost visible at the end of the lawn, reciting the story by heart.

> But in the farthest corner of the garden it was still winter, and in it was standing a little boy. He was so small he could not reach up to the branches of the tree, and he was wandering all round it, crying and crying.
> 'Climb up! little boy,' said the tree and it bent its branches down as low as it could; but the little boy was too tiny.

Oscar looked to heaven, but there was no help there. Clouds were gathering. A sudden wind blew the willows, and stirred the smooth surface of the river.

CHAPTER 9

*The world is a stage, but the play is
badly cast.*

THE OPENING of *A Woman of No Importance* approached, and
Oscar spent more and more time at the rehearsals.

As Lord Illingworth and Mrs Allonby brought Act One to
a close on-stage, under the direction of the actor-manager,
Herbert Beerbohm Tree, Oscar, Ada and Ross watched from
the stalls.

'Shall we go into tea?' asked Tree playing Illingworth.
'Do you like such simple pleasures?' responded Mrs Allonby
with a question of her own.

'I adore simple pleasures. They are the last refuge of the
complex. But, if you wish, let us stay here. Yes, let us stay
here. The Book of Life begins with a man and a woman in a
garden.'

'It ends with Revelations.'

Ada laughed broadly, but Oscar was not amused. He
rose, calling out for permission to address the actors.

'Mr Tree . . . may I? I'm delighted you find my lines
funny, of course. But please don't try to make people laugh

with them. They should sound completely spontaneous and natural, as though people spoke like that all the time.'

Having given his direction, Oscar smiled and retreated back to his stall while Tree conferred with the actors.

'You should break with Bosie more often, Oscar,' said Ada with an arch smile. 'Then we'd have more of your natural and spontaneous plays.'

Oscar smiled back, but not without difficulty.

'Bosie was envious,' said Ross. 'That's why he stopped Oscar working.'

'Robbie – please –' said Oscar, 'that's not true –'

'Of course it is,' Ross countered. 'His poems aren't nearly as good as you pretend, and he knows it. He's just a shallow little . . .'

Ada archly completed the thought, 'Rivulet!'

There was a profound silence, which Oscar broke apologetically.

'Bosie is a child – a vulnerable child. He needs love.'

'Oh, we all need love,' said Ada. 'But which of us can give it?'

Ross, looking carefully at Oscar, saw something that appalled him. 'Oscar, you're not – you're not seeing him again?'

Oscar chose to appear absorbed in what was happening on the stage.

'Oh, my God!' Ross turned to Ada, who shrugged.

'Love!' she said. 'That is spontaneous and natural. Alas.'

Bosie was indeed back.

In their Savoy Hotel suite, Oscar lay on the couch holding Bosie's head to his chest. He could barely move.

His skin felt tight and unnatural. It was as if a mask of despair were engraved in his face.

'I can't bear scenes,' Oscar sighed deeply. 'They kill me. They wreck the loveliness of life. Of our life. When you're angry, you look so cruel, so ugly, your lips –'

'I didn't mean those things.' Bosie stopped him. Then he sat up, looking directly at Oscar. 'When I get angry – everything goes round in my head – We're all the same in my family. We're terribly melodramatic.' He paused, then with a sense of profound loathing said, 'It's the bad Douglas blood.'

It was as near to an apology as Bosie could summon.

Oscar looked at him, shaking his head, 'I wish I could give you up. You're worse than cigarettes.'

Bosie placed his hand over Oscar's, 'There's nothing I wouldn't do for you. You know that. If you were to die – I shouldn't want to go on living. You make me realise – till I met you, I literally had no soul.'

Bosie leaned in to Oscar. Oscar took him in his arms, too moved to speak.

After a time, Bosie pulled back.

'I brought you a present,' he said, brightening.

Bosie got up, walked to the door and opened it, almost coquettishly. He looked at Oscar for dramatic effect, then disappeared round the corner, only to reappear moments later accompanied by a handsome young man of about eighteen, with a refined public school appearance and bearing.

Bosie bowed like a magician presenting a trick.

Oscar was briefly astounded, perhaps even horrified.

Then he laughed with delight, as Bosie introduced his gift.

'Say hello to Philip.'

Ross was very annoyed with Oscar when he heard about the escapade with Philip Dannay. Dannay was the son of an army colonel, and thus subject to public scrutiny in a way that others of Oscar's lads were not.

Ross bearded him in the drawing room at Tite Street.

Trying to sound the older and wiser man, he said, quite simply, 'Philip's too young.'

'Why? He's willing,' replied Oscar. 'As he tells me you've proved for yourself. Most satisfactorily.'

Oscar affected an arch calmness he did not feel at all.

'I am discreet,' said Ross, now totally exasperated. 'But Bosie — Oscar, you must understand. Philip's father is one of these purple-faced colonels who make the empire safe for English business. He's tried to make Philip tell him the whole story. And he has done, almost. He's kept your name out of it so far, but —'

'You're only cross because you wanted to keep Philip for yourself,' said Oscar, knowing that this wasn't true. 'I must be with young people, Robbie. They're so frank and free and — They make me feel young myself.'

'That's all very well, but what would you say if someone wanted to go to bed with your son?'

Oscar stopped cold in surprise and shock.

'Cyril's eight!'

'What will you say when he's eighteen?'

Oscar took time to consider this seriously. He had never before applied his own standards to his children, had never thought of them as adults with a life and destiny of their own.

The answer turned out to be easier than he expected, and

within a few seconds he was able to conclude with the strength of genuine conviction, 'Nothing. He must do as his nature dictates. As I only wish I'd done.'

'But discreetly. Bosie, of course, is far too grand and well-born for that. He wants everyone to know. You do realise, if Philip's father had taken this to court, Bosie and I would both have got two years? Hard labour. Fortunately, Philip would have got six months himself or his father –'

'Philip?' interrupted Oscar.

'It's the only thing that's stopping the colonel going to the police. He doesn't want his son publicly disgraced for ever.'

'Of course,' said Oscar, 'one man loving another in this country would bring the British Empire to its knees!'

'Well – the empire sends single men to places like Gujarat with their house-boys and serving maids and kitchen totos, and expects them to live chastely and lay down the moral law. Of course they have the usual run of human appetites, and they succumb in the usual manner to temptation. But if the general public knew what they actually get up to – there'd be no moral credibility left. So, yes,' stated Ross with some finality, 'sexual discretion is essential to the empire.'

'What a lot you suddenly know about the empire.'

'I'm Canadian, remember?' There was a silence. 'And now I must go to Switzerland. My family say I must go abroad for a while.'

Trying to make light of it, Oscar cried out, 'Switzerland! My poor dear Robbie!'

The very idea of an extended exile from his beloved London, whether self-imposed or not, struck Oscar as outrageous. It was not to be considered. The social and political issues Ross was presenting were an unwanted intrusion into Oscar's romantic model, but he had to admit that he had been dimly aware of these things all along. It was all so pedestrian . . . and sad.

'Bosie must go somewhere too,' Ross warned. 'And if he doesn't want to spend the rest of his life with all the other high-born English sodomites in Florence and Capri – well, he's going to have to mend his ways.'

Oscar looked at him, almost relieved to hear this.

'Think of it as a piece of luck,' Ross continued. 'You needed an excuse to break with Bosie.'

Oscar turned very sad, acknowledging the truth of Ross's observation.

'Yes, well – we couldn't go on like that, of course.'

Ross looked at him quizzically.

Oscar returned the look and nodded, 'It's over. And this time, I mean it.'

He did mean it. Yet he also felt an overwhelming loneliness. 'But what shall I do without you, Robbie?'

At Lady Queensberry's house, two carriages waited; one was piled high with luggage, the other ready for its sole passenger.

Bosie and his mother walked slowly through the house towards the front door. He was dressed for travelling.

'Egypt is lovely at this time of year,' she said 'but you mustn't idle your time away.'

'Mother –'

'And I want you to promise me something.'

They stopped and faced one another.

'Not to write to Oscar Wilde.'

'I can't do that.'

'Bosie —'

For once Bosie was completely genuine, as he turned to his mother and said, 'I love Oscar.'

Lady Queensberry opened her mouth, too horrified to speak.

'I love him as a disciple loves his teacher,' added Bosie.

'But he's not fit to teach anything,' she insisted, sputtering. 'He's evil!'

'Do you really think your own son could love someone evil? I just wish I could love Oscar as loyally, devotedly, unselfishly and purely as he loves me.'

Lady Queensberry could say nothing more to him.

'But I'm not as good as he is. I probably never will be.' Bosie kissed his mother. 'Goodbye.'

He turned and walked away.

Lady Queensberry watched the door close behind him. She heard the carriages clatter off, with their baggage and her son.

She remained in place, listening, for an awfully long time.

CHAPTER 10

*And the Giant's heart melted as he
looked out. 'How selfish I have been!'
he said. Now I know why the Spring
would not come here. I will put that
little boy on top of the tree, and I will
knock down the wall, and my garden
shall be the children's playground for
ever and ever. He was really very sorry
for what he had done.*

CHRISTMAS WAS A very special time that year.
There was a tree with a fairy on top, and a happy
family party with all the traditional trimmings. At table, the
children sang a special rendition of 'We Wish You a Merry
Christmas' that they had rehearsed for the occasion. There
were crackers to pull and stories to tell. Constance, Cyril
and Vyvyan had their beloved giant home for the holiday.

It was time for Oscar and Constance to put the boys to
bed and kiss them goodnight. There was only one story
they wanted to hear, and Oscar recited it for them, up the
stairs to the nursery, into their beds and far into their
dreams.

'So he crept downstairs and opened the front door quite softly, and went out into the garden. The little boy did not run away, for his eyes were so full of tears that he did not see the Giant coming. And the Giant stole up behind him and took him gently in his hand, and put him up into the tree. And the tree broke at once into blossom, and the birds came and sang on it, and the little boy stretched out his two arms and flung them round the Giant's neck and kissed him.'

So much for idyllic holidays. A few days later, Bosie, followed by porters carrying his luggage, rushed through reception at the Savoy and ran up the stairs . . . directly into Oscar's arms.

They hugged deliriously.

'I don't care what people think,' Bosie professed, laughing like a child. 'I don't care what they say. I love you. It's all that matters to me in the world. It was agony, being away from you. I couldn't bear it, Oscar. So – here I am.'

At that moment, the porters arrived with the luggage. They stood and stared at the oblivious couple.

'Oh, Bosie. You're my catastrophe, my doom. Everyone says so, even me.'

When John Sholto Douglas, eighth Marquess of Queensberry, came to the Café Royal for lunch the next day, he missed seeing Oscar and his son sitting together at their preferred central table.

Nor did they at first see him, wrapped up as they were in a cocoon of renewed intimacy.

Before ordering, Oscar handed Bosie a small parcel.

'I thought you might like something to celebrate your return.'

Bosie unwrapped the box eagerly, revealing a pair of emerald cuff-links.

'Oh, Oscar!' He was as pleased as a child.

'When I saw them in the window, they begged me on their knees to make them yours.'

'I'll put them on now! They're superb!'

Under Oscar's proud and admiring eye, Bosie undid the links he had on, replacing them with the new ones. When this was done, he looked over at Oscar with that fond, serious look he cultivated. He reached his hands to Oscar's face as if to remove some crumb or smudge of dirt on his cheek, turning the gesture into a highly public caress which had the added benefit of displaying the new cuff-links.

The moment was shattered by an altercation a few tables away, as Queensberry raised his voice to a waiter.

'No, no, no, no! I'll sit there,' he said pointing to a different place. 'I want a proper table.'

He was not a large man, but his bearing was brusque and bellicose enough for three men of greater stature. His eyes flashed as he spoke, and his long mutton-chops exhibited a life of their own as he ground his teeth and growled at all about him.

The head waiter approached solicitously. 'Is there something wrong?'

'Of course there is. This young fool wants me to sit by the service door.'

'Excuse him, my Lord. He's new. He didn't know who you were. This way, please . . .'

Slightly mollified, Queensberry sat at his new table and demanded a menu.

Bosie stared across the room in horror. 'Oh, my God. My father!'

He rose from his seat.

'Bosie, you're not going to flee?' asked Oscar. Oddly, he couldn't tell from Bosie's expression whether he was distracted or determined. Either possibility seemed extremely dangerous.

Bosie did not reply.

Oscar watched with apprehension, peering out from behind his menu to avoid detection, as Bosie began walking directly towards his father. Queensberry, thinking him a waiter, did not at first look up.

'I'll have the pea soup, then the salmon.'

'Will you have it with us, Papa?'

'Bosie!' His father was startled.

'I'm lunching with Oscar Wilde. Will you join us?'

Queensberry paused in amazement, then began to launch into one of his tirades.

'I told you never to see that vile cur again.'

'He's not vile or a cur, he's utterly delightful. Come and see,' pleaded Bosie. 'How do you know what he's like when you've never met him? Come on, Papa. You're not a man to be influenced by other people's opinions.'

This hit home.

Queensberry got up stiffly.

Oscar was very conscious of everyone watching as father and son made their way towards him, across the restaurant, a waiter bringing up the rear with Queensberry's chair.

'Oscar, you've never met my father, have you?'

Oscar rose. 'Lord Queensberry.'

The two men shook hands, then sat.

'Bosie has told me so much about your exploits on the

race-track,' Oscar began pleasantly,' I've never heard such bad luck as yours with the Grand National.'

Queensberry looked surprised.

'Bosie says you could have won, but your cousin wouldn't let you ride the horse.'

Somewhat taken aback, Queensberry was melting already, trying with difficulty to maintain his gruff and belligerent stance.

'Bloody fool said I was too old,' he mumbled as if he did not want to be caught speaking. 'But you're never too old. And I'd ridden Old Joe on the gallops. Came in at forty to one.'

Bosie watched Oscar's tactfulness appreciatively.

'No horse could ever have carried me round the jumps I fear,' said Oscar. 'What are you eating?'

'Pea soup, and salmon.'

'Then I shall join you. Spring is the time for salmon, isn't it? Though I always think it tastes so much nicer if you've caught it yourself.'

'You fish?' Queensberry was wide-eyed with surprise.

'I used to,' said Oscar genially. 'When I lived in Ireland. My father had the most charming hunting lodge on an island in a lake. Do you know the West of Ireland?'

'Not really.' Queensberry thought about this for a moment then leaned in towards Oscar, confidentially. 'Whereabouts, exactly?'

Some considerable time later, Bosie the restaurant alone, smiling to himself.

And later still, when nearly all the other lunchers had left, the two remained, smoking – Queensberry a cigar and

Oscar a cigarette – and discussing Christianity over their brandy. The Marquess had a long-standing reputation for atheism and iconoclasm, and had been denied re-admission to the House of Lords on the grounds that he had publicly denied the existence of God.

'I believe in God,' Queensberry said firmly. 'Oh, yes, I believe in God. I call him The Inscrutable.'

'Well he is inscrutable, of course.'

'The Christians, they pretend to know who God is and how he works. Well, I have no time for that sort of tomfoolery. If you don't know what something is, you should stand up and say so, not go around pretending you believe in a lot of mumbojumbo.'

'I can believe in anything,' said Oscar after thinking a moment, 'provided it's incredible. That's why I intend to die a Catholic, though I couldn't possibly live as one.'

Queensberry eyed him suspiciously, but Oscar continued. 'Catholicism is such a romantic religion. It has saints and sinners. The Church of England only has respectable people who believe in respectability. You get to be a bishop, not by what you believe, but by what you don't.'

'Ha, ha!' Queensberry burst out in a staccato laugh of agreement. 'That's true enough.'

'It's the only Church where the sceptic stands at the altar, and St Thomas the doubter is the prince of the apostles. No, I couldn't possibly die in the Church of England.'

Queensberry leaned forward, his expression dead serious, 'Where do you stand on cremation?' he demanded.

'I'm not sure I have a position.'

'I'm for it,' said Queensberry. 'I wrote a poem. "When I am dead, cremate me," that's how it begins.' He paused for effect, then began again in what he no doubt considered a

more poetic manner. ' "When I am dead, cremate me."
What do you think about that for an opening line?'

'It's . . . challenging.'

'I'm a challenging sort of man. That's why people don't
like me. Don't go along with the ordinary ways of
thinking.'

Queensberry returned to his cigar with a self-satisfied
expression.

'Then we're exactly alike,' said Oscar.

To this there was, oddly, no argument from Queensberry.

Oscar asked, 'Another glass of brandy?' and poured them
each a generous helping from the crystal decanter. 'I find
that alcohol taken in sufficient quantities can produce all the
effects of drunkenness.'

'You were there for ages,' Bosie commented to his father
later, the suggestion of a petulant grin on his face. 'You
stayed talking till after four.'

They were at the stables, where Queensberry was looking
at horses, feeling their legs, watching as they were trotted
up and down for him. He was at home here, amidst the
animals he loved, the machinery of hunting and racing all
about. He was less comfortable with people, where his
business tended towards the litigious or the downright
violent. But his was not a casual or random brutality. This
was, after all, the man who had single-handedly changed
the course of boxing by introducing, both to England and
America, a system of rules that insured a far greater degree
of fairness than had ever been customary.

The Marquess was perhaps least comfortable in the
presence of his son.

Uppermost on his mind, besides the influence of Wilde, was Bosie's failure to appear for his June exams, an event which had led to disfavour on the part of Magdalen College and a furious withdrawal from Oxford by Bosie.

Both men tried to keep calm, but both were also aware that a fight was inevitable.

Bosie chewed a nail and laughed around his hand, 'I knew you'd like him once you'd met him.'

'Well – Well – he's got charm, I admit that.' Queensberry frowned. 'But that's bad. Men shouldn't be charming. Disgusting.' His attention turned towards the groom, 'Don't think much of his action. Let's see the bay,' then returned to Bosie. 'Mind you, Wilde's no fool. Talks wonderfully, really wonderfully.' Again he frowned. 'But that means nothing when what he says is such – such rot. And worse than rot. Evil. Which is why I insist you stop seeing him forthwith.'

'Insist? What's that supposed to mean?'

'It means I cut off your allowance if you don't do as I say.'

Queensberry watched as a new horse was brought round.

'Trot him up and down,' he shouted, suddenly striding forth across the stablyard with great energy, his riding crop in hand. It was all Bosie could do to keep up.

'You wasted your time at Oxford,' Queensberry's voice terrorised the horses, 'pretending you were going into the Foreign Office – which thank God you didn't, when the Jew queer Rosebery can become Foreign Secretary and bugger all the juniors – including your brother –'

'Papa, that's all lies!' Bosie shouted back, actually shocked.

'You spent your whole time writing obscene poems –'

'My poems aren't obscene!'

'They're in the manner of Wilde. That's filthy enough for me.'

'Have you ever actually read Oscar's poems?' asked Bosie.

'I wouldn't sully my mind with perverted trash like that.' Queensberry turned his anger to the horse. 'Tell him to pick his feet up. He's not straight!' he shouted at the groom.

'Are you calling Oscar a pervert?' shouted Bosie, 'Because that's libellous!'

But Queensberry, veteran of many a lawsuit, was too sharp to be caught so easily, and had his position already worked out. 'I'm not saying he *is* one. I'm saying he's *posing* as one. Which is even worse. His wife's divorcing him. Did you know that? For sodomy.'

'That's completely untrue!'

'I hope it is. Because if I thought it was true, I'd shoot him on sight,' said Queensberry, looking quite capable of it. He took control of himself, and walked deliberately up to Bosie. The force of his attack caused Bosie involuntarily to back up a couple of steps.

'You will cease to see Wilde, or I will cut you off without a penny.' With that, Queensberry spun on his heel and walked away.

Bosie turned white with rage.

'As though I wanted your money!' he yelled at full volume. 'What little you've got left from your tarts.'

'How dare you speak to your father like that!' Queensberry shouted back from across the yard.

Bosie laughed bitterly, 'What a funny little man you are.'

He began to run, in no particular direction, his rage driving him about the yard like a billiard ball out of control.

'Bosie! Come back here, you filthy-minded little sissy!'

'You're absurd!' called Bosie, and he disappeared into the darkness of a stable enclosure.

'And you're nothing but a bumboy!'

'You're pathetic!!' Bosie's voice echoed from the darkness. Then a burst of light flashed through the stable as he opened a door on the other side, emerged into brightest day, and was gone from sight.

'Bosie!!!' screamed Queensberry furiously.

It had long been too late for reconciliations.

CHAPTER 11

Actions are the first tragedy in life,
words are the second. Words are
perhaps the worst. Words are merciless.

IT WAS JUNE 1894, and a fine day in the park. People rode horses or strolled along in pairs and small groups. It was all quite tranquil, except for an area in the immediate vicinity of Bosie and Oscar, and here people were inclined to go round about, for Bosie was attempting to twirl a shining silver revolver in something akin to the manner of a professional gunslinger.

He wasn't terribly good at it. He stalked about, pointing the gun at various objects, with a dangerous glint in his eye. His head thrust forward and his back arched belligerently.

It struck Oscar that Bosie looked like his father. The thought did not inspire confidence, and Oscar was feeling very apprehensive, as were the bystanders on all sides.

'I'm a bloody good shot,' shouted Bosie, 'better than he is! I'll shoot him through the heart, if he threatens me!'

'Hadn't you better use a silver bullet, then?' Oscar tried against hope to keep things light.

Bosie aimed, and fired at a passing pigeon. The bullet

splintered the branch of a tree. A horse bolted, out of control.

'There's one for the Black Douglas!' Bosie shouted.

'For God's sake, Bosie!' Oscar's alarm grew with each shot.

Bosie fired off more shots, unpredictably turning this way and that, and cutting a swathe through the dispersing crowd. He was laughing like a madman.

'There's one for his liver and one for his lights and one for his stinking rotten soul!'

'Bosie!' Oscar put his right arm around the boy's shoulder, and wrested the pistol from him. Bosie looked up into Oscar's face, his expression the twisted mask of a small spoiled child.

Bosie lurched against him. 'I'll save one for myself.'

Oscar felt pity for Bosie, but also fear for both of them. Bosie's extravagant outburst had rocked his own foundations. There were suddenly real ogres in his garden, when all along he'd thought they were merely fantastical inventions. He looked around nervously, and he saw no refuge, no safe harbour, only the startled condemnation of the good people of London.

Bosie suddenly shivered, as if terrified of what he had done or almost done. He slumped into Oscar's arms, head hidden against his chest.

'My own father. He wants to kill me.'

Later, Oscar lay curled up at the far end of the sofa. Bosie lay over him, and wrapped his body around him, his cheek against Oscar's back. Oscar felt comforted by Bosie's presence, but not consoled. In watching Bosie's fit of rage earlier, he had learned something about himself. For the first time, he was able to understand that the pristine vision he had held when he married, the happy self-portrait of his soul, the uncluttered destiny, were all gone, and had been gone for a long time. In their place was a void, and there was nothing he could do about it. Everything was out of his hands.

'My life is everything I ever wanted. I have fame. I have recognition. With two plays about to open in London, I may even have money. The world is at my command. But I can't command myself. I can't command my feelings for you.'

They lay like that, still and mostly silent, for the rest of the long afternoon.

CHAPTER 12

One can always be kind to people
about whom one cares nothing.

As THE SUMMER of 1894 declined into autumn, the Wildes rented a small house on the Esplanade at Worthing.

Worthing Pier had something for everyone in those days. One could promenade on the boardwalk, or swim, or fish.

At one end of the pier, Oscar and the boys fished, while Constance watched and encouraged their efforts from under a broad-brimmed hat. They seemed a very happy family group, although Constance and the children were scheduled to return to London the following day, in anticipation of the beginning of the autumn term.

The boys were nine and eight now, and in very high spirits. Oscar baited their hooks, carefully showing them how to do it. His concentration flagged from time to time, though, and he felt congested.

He sneezed violently into a handkerchief.

'I don't think we have anything for our table tonight . . . no luck.'

'I think I'd better stay,' said Constance. 'You're getting a cold.'

'No, no, I'm all right,' Oscar insisted. 'Let's get the boys some ices. Boys, stay and look after Nanny.'

Oscar and Constance strolled off up the boardwalk.

'I can take the boys to the dentist on Thursday, on their way back to boarding school,' said Constance.

'But the whole point of them having dentistry now,' said Oscar, 'is so they can stuff themselves with sweets for a week before we lose them.'

Constance laughed. Oscar sneezed.

'Are you quite sure – ?' she asked.

'Bosie'll look after me.' Oscar sneezed yet again, and shielded his eyes from the glare of the sun.

Rarely far from Oscar, even at Worthing, Bosie leaned against the railing at the other end of the Pier, where it was not uncommon for young men, some of them quite naked, to gather for water sports. He watched a group of these dive from a pontoon, horse about, and otherwise disport themselves.

Oscar could barely make him out from a distance.

His smile was jaunty, and his interest was keen.

In time Oscar was indeed confined to bed with flu.

He was feeling very sorry for himself, and resentful that Bosie had apparently abandoned him, when he heard the front door slam below and Bosie's footsteps come running up the stairs. His voice echoed in the hall outside.

'Oscar! Oscar! Get your clothes on – quick! I've got a present for you!'

Bosie appeared in the doorway, flushed with drink.

'Oh, God,' he said with a look of disgust, 'you're not still seedy, are you?'

'Bosie, where have you been?' complained Oscar. 'I've had no one to talk to, no one to look after me –'

'Don't be so pathetic, I've found you the divinest boy!'

'Bosie, you promised Constance you'd –'

'Bugger Constance! I'm not your nanny!'

Bosie walked across the room quickly. He was frenetic and furious, under a kind of studied nonchalance. There were people waiting for him.

'Come on,' he said, 'we're going out.'

He took some cigarettes from a box on the dressing table and filled his case. He wasn't going to have his plans for the evening thwarted.

'Bosie, please,' said Oscar.

'You look such an idiot, lying there. Revolting. Have you forgoteen how to wash?' Oscar could see the cruel thrust of Bosie's jaw in the mirror, and he was shattered by this sudden and unprovoked attack.

He tried to compose himself, 'As a matter of fact I'm dying for a glass of water.'

'Well, help yourself. You know where the jug is.'

'Bosie – darling –'

'It stinks in here. You'll be wanting me to empty your chamber pot next,' he said, making a disgusted face. He found a bottle of cologne, and proceeded to douse himself with it.

'I emptied your chamber-pot,' Oscar said. 'I looked after you.'

Bosie turned, his eyes flashing.

'Well, I'm not looking after you. Not now. You don't

interest me, not when you're ill. You're just a boring middle-aged man with a blocked-up nose.'

Vulnerable as he was, Oscar could not help but see himself as Bosie apparently saw him, and he was appalled. He could even hear the whine in his voice as he pleaded, 'Bosie – dearest boy –'

'Shut up!' snapped Bosie, turning to the mirror to smooth his hair delicately with his palm. 'Dearest boy, darling Bosie – it doesn't mean anything! You don't love me. The only person you've ever loved is yourself. You like me, you lust after me, you go about with me, because I've got a title, that's all. You like to write about dukes and duchesses, but you know nothing about them. You're the biggest snob I've ever met. And you think you're so daring because you fuck the occasional boy!'

This was unbearable to Oscar.

'Bosie, please – you're killing me –'

'You'll just about do when you're at your best. You're amusing, very amusing, but when you're not at your best, you're no one.'

Primed, sleek, well groomed, Bosie found a few loose coins, placed them in his pocket, and started towards the door.

'All I asked for was a glass of water.'

'For Christ's sake!' Bosie stopped by the door, took the glass jug, and threw it to the floor with all the force he could muster. 'There you are then!' he screamed. 'Now will you shut up about the fucking water!' His sleekness was suddenly gone. His violent movements had sent his hair into the air, and it was standing in spikes. He looked to Oscar like a harpy or a Medusa, standing there, shaking with fury and quite mad. Oscar became genuinely frightened of him.

'There are two boys waiting out there.' Bosie said. He was quieter now, no longer shouting, and that, if anything, made him appear even more terrifying. 'If you're not coming, I'll fuck both of them myself. I'll take them to the Grand and fuck them in front of the whole fucking hotel. And I'll send you the bill.'

He left.

Oscar lay there, and underneath the self-pity and the momentary self-loathing, he began to understand something. He knew now that it would always be like this with Bosie.

There was little point in staying on holiday in his condition, so Oscar returned home. At Tite Street, although still under the weather and well wrapped up, Oscar was at least able to have company.

Ross was a ministering angel to him, caring for Oscar in every conceivable way, encouraging him to speak openly and unburden himself.

He held a lighted match to a snifter of brandy until it was well-warmed, then brought the glass to Oscar.

'Drink this,' he said, then helped himself to a drink. As Oscar carried on his *apologia pro vita sua* in an uncharacteristically halting manner.

'His father bullies him – his mother spoils him, then berates him for being spoiled – neither of them gives him any real love. They're torturing him. And what's truly dreadful is – when he can't bear it, and – and – has one of his – his – he becomes exactly like his father. And he hates himself for that and –'

'You're too kind about him, Oscar.' Ross sat in an armchair close by. His kindness and concern were a warm wrap for Oscar.

'You can't be too kind about someone who's been so – so hurt. Yet – if I go on trying to come between Bosie and his father's wrath – they'll destroy me.'

'Bosie's quite capable of destroying you on his own. Look how much you wrote while he was away. Two wonderful plays which will run for years – back comes Bosie – what have you written since?'

This was a sore subject with Oscar, and not something he cared to admit. He became quiet.

'Oscar,' continued Ross. 'You know how much I . . .love and admire you – but you're throwing your genius away – for what?'

Oscar replied bitterly, 'It's highly ironic. Queensberry thinks Bosie and I are locked in nightly embrace, when in reality we've been the purest model of Greek love since –' Oscar paused, while Ross looked at him, intrigued. 'Bosie doesn't like doing it with me. I've loved him, I've educated him –'

'But he's never grown up,' concluded Ross. 'And he never will.'

Oscar made up his mind. Ross's presence and encouragement had given him the strength.

'I'm not taking him back, Robbie. Not again. I can't.'

Ross smiled. In view of history, he had great difficulty believing this.

But Oscar was very sad.

'I've been very foolish, very fond, and now – I must grow up myself.'

'Oh, please don't do that,' Ross comforted him. 'You're an artist. And artists are always children at heart.'

Oscar gave him a smile of genuine gratitude.

'Oh, Robbie – I sometimes wonder whether – you and I – ?'

The thought was left hanging as Arthur entered with a newspaper under his arm. He bent down and whispered in Oscar's ear, gave him the newspaper, and left. Oscar opened it and read rapidly. He was horrified by the news.

'My God! Francis Douglas!'

'What?'

'Bosie's brother! He's been found shot! He's dead.'

Oscar handed over the paper.

'But he's just got engaged, he . . .'

'Bosie! Oh, poor, poor Bosie!' wailed Oscar. 'He'll be utterly distraught!'

Oscar was right.

In Lady Queensberry's drawing room, Bosie was weeping. He was draped over a sofa arm, his face hidden from Oscar and the world.

Oscar noticed that the lad had assumed a posture quite similar to a nearby statue by Rodin obviously depicting some sort of sorrow. He sat close by, trying to comfort Bosie without intruding too rudely on his grief.

'Francis was a wonderful young man. He had the world before him. It was a terrible accident.'

Bosie shook his head, and murmured into his sleeve, 'He killed himself.'

Oscar felt compelled to keep talking, to offer some more positive version of the facts.

'He had everything to live for. He had you, he had your mother, his fiancée – everyone loved him.'

'It was my father. He drove him to it.'

There was a new tone in Bosie's voice, harsher than anything Oscar had heard from him before.

'I'm sure your father's as upset as everyone else.'

'He's not.' Bosie turned his head just enough so he could look up at Oscar. 'He says it's a judgement on Rosebery. And my mother. And me and you.'

Oscar had no answer to that.

'We've got to stop him, Oscar,' said Bosie, sitting up, 'before he drives the whole family to suicide.'

Oscar took Bosie's head in his arms, and held him fast.

'Bosie – Bosie, I promise you – I shall never let him hurt you again, I promise.'

'That's not enough.' Bosie reached for Oscar's hand, but his voice was cold. 'I want him stopped. I want the whole world to know what he's done, what an evil man he is.'

CHAPTER 13

I choose my friends for their good looks, my acquaintances for their good character, and my enemies for their good intellect. A man cannot be too careful in the choice of his enemies.

As the opening dates of *An Ideal Husband* and *The Importance of Being Earnest* approached, Oscar's name was everywhere. Talk of his reviews and other writings were on everyone's lips.

One mild and sunny afternoon in December 1894, Oscar emerged from the Haymarket Theatre, where *An Ideal Husband* was in rehearsal, not knowing that Alfred Wood was waiting outside the stage door with Charles Parker. They seemed nervous in a predatory sort of way, and kept themselves out of sight until they spotted Oscar.

Oscar called out to the stagedoor keeper, 'Till tomorrow, Johnny!'

With a hearty 'Goodbye, sir,' from Johnny, the stage door slammed heavily shut, and Oscar proceeded quickly down the street.

As they'd been waiting on the opposite side of the door

from the direction Oscar was now taking, Wood and Parker
had to run to catch him up.

'Hello, Oscar!' cried Wood.

'Alfred! How nice to see you.' Oscar saw Parker behind
Wood, 'And Charlie. You're looking well.' At once he
guessed that they were after something, and he had a pretty
good idea what that might be.

He instantly became geniality itself.

'I'm afraid I'm busy this evening, but we must have
dinner again soon, shall we?'

'It's not a question of dinner,' said Wood. 'I've got a
letter of yours. To Lord Alfred.'

He showed Oscar the letter, but from a distance, keeping
it well out of his reach.

Parker elaborated, with a smirk, 'It's nice, Oscar . . .
beautiful. Lips like roses . . . the madness of kisses in ancient
Greece.'

'Oh, then, I expect it's one of my prose poems.'

This was not at all what the boys were expecting, but
Wood persisted.

'There's a gentleman has offered me sixty pounds for it.'

'Then you must accept, Alfred. I've never received so
large a sum for a prose work of that length in all my life.
Tell your friend I'm delighted that someone in England
values my work so highly.'

Wood mumbled, 'Well, he's gone away ...'

'He's in the country,' added Parker.

Oscar assumed these were euphemisms for a prison
sentence.

'Well, I'm sure he'll be back soon.'

Thus dismissing the boys, he began to walk away.

They ran after him. 'Oscar! Oscar!'

As Oscar stopped, Wood, looking down, almost ashamed, took hold of Oscar's sleeve.

'Look, you couldn't let us have something – I'm a bit short at the moment, and – you know –'

Oscar paused, and then took a coin from his waistcoat pocket.

'Of course, of course. Here's half a sovereign. Now mind you look after that letter. Lord Alfred's going to publish it in sonnet form in his new magazine.'

As Oscar once again sauntered off, the boys looked at one another in dismay.

'Fuck's sake!' exploded Parker.

Again they ran after him, calling his name.

Oscar stopped yet again.

When they were face to face, Wood said sheepishly, It's no good trying to rent you, you just laugh at us.' He reached out and offered Oscar the letter, 'Here.'

'Well, thank you, Alfred.'

Oscar examined the offending piece of paper, which was very grubby.

'You haven't taken very good care of it.'

'It's been through a few hands,' admitted Wood. 'He can be very careless, Lord Alfred.'

Oscar looked at Wood seriously, taking in the information. Then he laughed, 'What a wonderfully wicked life you lead!'

Giving Wood another half-sovereign, Oscar tut-tutted, 'You boys! You boys!' as he resumed his journey down the street.

He was pleased with himself. After all, any situation could be handled if one had the wit and didn't cave in to pressure.

Oscar was on other people's minds as well.

At the Café Royal, Lord Queensberry shoved his way in past waiting customers, and stared belligerently around. The head waiter approached him.

'Table, my lord?'

'Is Lord Alfred here? And that shit and sod Wilde?'

Taken aback, the head waiter said, 'No, my lord, not tonight.'

'Bugger must be at Kettner's.'

Later, after several other stops, the scene was repeated at a hotel, as Queensberry came barging in and up to the reception desk.

'Is my son here?'

The manager looked at him blankly.

'Lord Alfred Douglas!' insisted Queensberry, speaking as if to an idiot, 'Is he staying here?'

'No, sir, he's not.'

'What about Wilde?'

'No, sir.'

'If I find they have been staying here, I'll give you the biggest whipping of your life!' shouted Queensberry. Then he turned on his heels and left.

Meanwhile, upstairs, Bosie was in bed with Alfred Wood, fucking enthusiastically in the missionary position. Wood had a pillow under his bum and his legs in the air.

Oscar smoked a cigarette, and watched Bosie's buttocks going up and down. This kind of ménage, with Oscar relegated to the role of observer, was a more and more common occurence with them.

Bosie paused in his activity long enough to glance over at

Oscar and give him an impish grin of complicity. Oscar smiled back, of course, hiding his pain. He was not totally sure why he was here, only that he seemed to have no choice in the matter.

Bosie climaxed loudly, waited a moment, and rolled off. Wood pulled the covers over them both.

Champagne and glasses were arranged haphazardly on the table, and Oscar began to pour some. 'I expect you both need a drink after your exertions.' He saw Wood's eyes widen, and then Bosie giggled.

Oscar turned.

The hotel manager was standing in the doorway, with a floor waiter looking excitedly over his shoulder. In the noise and flush of the moment, none of the three had heard the passkey being used in the sitting room.

The manager took in the scene at a glance.

'I must ask you to leave, Mr Wilde.'

Oscar was shaken and embarrassed, but he showed none of it. He remained still, seated upright.

'My dear man, what are you talking about?' he said coolly.

'At once, please.'

'What's the matter?' chimed in Bosie. 'My father cracking the whip downstairs, is he?'

The manager gave Wood a curt nod to tell him to get up and get dressed, and Wood rapidly complied.

Bosie, though, stayed right where he was. He wasn't going to be pushed about by anyone.

'My lord —' began the manager again.

'Bosie —' Oscar spoke as well.

'You're not frightened of what this little man thinks, are you?' asked Bosie.

'I think,' said Oscar, 'the pleasures of the evening should be resumed elsewhere.'

After staring momentarily at Oscar, Bosie got up and started to dress. He was furious.

'You're such a coward. You say you despise convention, but you're the most conventional man I know.'

One of his emerald cuff-links fell to the floor. Bosie contemptuously kicked it under the bed.

'Come on, then,' Bosie sneered. 'If we're going, let's go!'

He walked out, still half dressed, followed by Wood and Oscar. The manager held the door, standing back as far as he could from the guilty trio.

The ruckus even followed Oscar home, to his inner sanctum. He was dining alone in his study at Tite Street, casually picking at his food, a fork in one hand and a book in the other, when he heard the front door opening, then sounds of commotion coming from the hallway.

It was Queensberry's voice raised in anger, with the servant Arthur unsuccessfully trying to hold him off. There were cries of 'Where is he?' and 'Excuse me, sir —'

Then Arthur entered the study, distraught. 'There's a gentleman —' he began to explain, when Queensberry burst into the room.

The Marquess flourished his riding whip, as he looked about the room with an expression of disgust. A little behind him stood his companion, a gnarled and cauliflower-eared boxer wearing a bowler hat.

'You. You listen to me,' Queensberry began in measured tones of barely contained rage. 'You're a bugger!'

Oscar rose, slowly and deliberately.

'I don't allow people to talk to me like that in my own

house, Lord Queensberry. Or anywhere else. I suppose you've come to apologise for the lies you've been spreading about me?'

'I've come to tell you to leave my son alone! You sodomite!'

Oscar turned inquiringly to the boxer, 'The Marquess seems very obsessed with other people's sexual activities. Has it anything to do with his new wife, I wonder? And the fact she's seeking a divorce for non-consummation?'

This left the boxer too flabbergasted to speak, and Queensberry white with rage.

'Unless you swear to have nothing more to do with Bosie,' he said. 'I shall go to Scotland Yard!'

'You can go to the devil! You and your —' Oscar glanced at the boxer. 'Who is this gargoyle?'

The boxer stared menacingly back.

'You're a queer and a — a — sham!' Queensberry sputtered. 'A poseur! If I catch you and Bosie together again I'll give you such a thrashing —'

Oscar chose to address the boxer, 'I believe Lord Queensberry once invented some rules for boxing. I've no idea what they are. But the Oscar Wilde rule is to shoot on sight. Now kindly leave my house.'

'You can shut up. I shall leave when I'm damned well ready,' shouted Queensberry, raising his whip in menacing fashion.

Without warning, Oscar strode up to Queensberry, grabbed the whip from him, and snapped it in two.

Queensberry was taken aback at this unexpected violence. He was clearly unused to being at the receiving end. He fired his last shot.

'It's a scandal, what you've been doing!'

'All the scandal is your own,' said Oscar. 'Your treatment of your wives. Your neglect of your children. And above all, your depraved insistence that they be as tyrannical and unloving as you are yourself. Arthur,' he continued, turning to the aghast servant, 'this is the Marquess of Queensberry, the most infamous brute and least tender father in London. Never let him in the house again.'

Arthur opened the door.

Not knowing how to make his retreat with dignity, Queensberry finally nodded to the boxer.

'Very well, then. Let's get out of this − stew.'

When they had gone, and Oscar was alone, he allowed his mask of cool control to slip.

He was trembling − with anger, as well as fear, as he returned to his chair. He lifted his wine glass, held it with both hands to steady his nerves, then took a deep draught of his wine.

A cold spell had hit London, and it was a particularly frigid Valentine's Day in 1895. But inside the St James's Theatre an eager crowd, warmed by keen anticipation and the odd toddy, were taking their seats for the opening night of *The Importance of Being Earnest.*

Lilies of the valley, the latest emblem of Wildean aesthetics, were sported in all the young men's buttonholes and on the dresses of Oscar's women friends. At earlier openings, it had been green carnations, an emblem of the ascendance of the artificial over nature, that prevailed. As Oscar substituted one fashion for another, what remained constant was the need for some sort of badge of member-ship in the elite club over which he ruled.

Among the excited throng were Constance, Ada, Speranza, Ross, Gray, Lady Mount-Temple and others.

Bosie was away in Algiers.

Outside the theatre, in the bitter cold, there was a sudden scuffle, as two policemen wrestled with Lord Queensberry and the boxer. The Marquess shouted obcenities, until finally the policemen managed to push him away from the stage door.

Queensberry grabbed a bundle from the boxer. He tore it open, and threw its contents at the officers, who became covered with bits of raw vegetables.

'I want you to give these to Oscar Wilde!' he screamed.

'Thank you, sir,' replied one of the policemen, trying to keep his composure, 'we'll take care of them.'

'I wanted to give it to him personally. As a bouquet.'

Again the policeman interfered, 'I dare say you did sir, but you're not going to.'

Thwarted, Queensberry turned away, frowning angrily and cursing under his breath, 'Cur! Sod!'

He marched down the street, his shoulder to the wind, then turned back a last time to the policemen.

'And a bugger!' he shouted. 'You remember that!'

The performance that night was certainly better for Queensberry's absence. As the play drew to its close, there was a huge roar of laughter. On-stage, Jack held the Army List. He put it down and spoke quite calmly to Gwendolen.

'I always told you, Gwendolen, my name was Ernest, didn't I? Well, it is Ernest after all. I mean it naturally is Ernest.'

Boisterous laughter erupted here, as Lady Bracknell picked up her cue.

'Yes, I remember now that the general was called Ernest. I knew I had some particular reason for disliking the name.'

There was another burst of laughter.

Ada thought the use of that name particularly amusing.

Beside her, however, Lady Mount-Temple had recognised herself and was not at all amused. She frowned in stern censure as Lady Bracknell continued to speak.

'Come, Gwendolen.'

'Ernest! My own Ernest!' this from Gwendolen, 'I felt from the first you could have no other name!'

'Gwendolen,' said Jack, 'it is a terrible thing for a man to find out suddenly that all his life he has been speaking nothing but the truth. Can you forgive me?'

'I can' said Gwendolen. 'For I feel that you are sure to change.'

Laughter again, as Jack moved to embrace his dear, 'My own one!'

And so the inevitable, hysterical finale resolved itself in a fit of romantic momentum, as Canon Chasuble, Miss Prism, Algernon and Jack all found their partners by turn.

'Laetitia!'

'Frederick! At last!'

'Cecily! At last!'

'Gwendolen! At last!'

Oscar watched from the wings as all three couples embraced and Lady Bracknell once again spoke.

'My nephew, you seem to be displaying signs of triviality.'

'On the contrary, Aunt Augusta,' replied Jack. 'I've now realised for the first time in my life the vital Importance of Being Earnest.'

And on this the curtain fell.

There was a storm of applause, then a standing ovation. George Alexander, the actor-manager, came backstage to lead Oscar on. Oscar put out his cigarette this time, and allowed himself to be pulled out on to the stage.

The applause was thunderous as he took his bow, bravos from every corner. From his vantage point, in front of the house, he could see all his friends, laughing and clapping.

There was no speech this time, just a few small bows to acknowledge the adulation of the crowd. As he let the waves of sound roll over him, Oscar simply stood in place and felt a degree of humility. He had no doubt that this was the finest moment of his life.

The stories about Oscar kept circulating, becoming more vivid by the day. In polite circles, as at the Albemarle Club, where Oscar had once been a valued member, his appearance was now met with stony silence or the hiss of whispers.

So much for the illusion of a man's privacy. It was at the Albermarle Club, that on 28 February Oscar received an envelope with a card inside. It had been delivered ten days earlier, he was told by Sidney Wright, the hall porter.

He returned to his suite at the Cadogan Hotel, where Ross took the card from him, and tried to decipher it under Bosie's tutelage. Slowly, carefully, he articulated syllable after syllable, ' "To Oscar Wilde – ponce, is it? Ponce and – somdomite?" '

' "Posing as a sodomite," ' Bosie corrected. When faced with a crisis, Bosie's behaviour was predictable. He mostly drank whisky, while walking about in a highly excited state. 'He's illiterate. Illiterate, ignorant –'

'It's hideous,' Oscar muttered. Then he got up and left the room.

'We've got him now!' shouted Bosie. 'He wrote it down and the porter read it. That makes it a public libel. Now we can take him to court.'

Appalled, Ross turned to Oscar, who was no longer there. He called after him, 'For God's sake, Oscar . . .' and followed him into the other room, 'Oscar, you mustn't do that, that'd be – I mean –'

Bosie appeared, and cut him off, 'We've just been waiting for a chance to get him in the dock and show the world what a swine and shit he's always been. To me and my mother, my brothers –'

'But he'll plead justification,' argued Ross. 'He'll call all the renters as witnesses for the defence.'

'Of course he won't,' countered Bosie. 'He doesn't know what a renter is.'

'No? I hear he's had detectives following you ever since you came back from Egypt.'

'He can't prove anything,' insisted Bosie. 'But we can. We can prove he's the vilest man that ever walked the earth.'

Seeing that he was getting nowhere arguing with Bosie, Ross turned to Oscar.

'Tear the card up, Oscar. Pretend you never got it.'

Bosie quickly pounced on the card, and put it away in his jacket for protection, 'Are you mad? That's our main piece of evidence!'

The two young men argued, while Oscar remained silent, retaining his composure whatever the cost. It was clear to him that he could not ignore the situation any longer, that he would have to take some sort of stand.

Bosie's and Ross's words took on the character of mere noise, a background to his deliberations. The actions were mildly comic, like a Punch and Judy show. Oscar tried to pay attention. Perhaps if he listened carefully, he would hear a clue as to what he was supposed to do about all this.

Ross tried to lay out his plan rationally, 'I'm sure, if Oscar went abroad for a few months, lived on his royalties while your father calms down – then you wrote something for the papers, explaining –'

'Whose side are you on?' said Bosie, looking sharply at Ross, while lighting a cigarette for Oscar.

'Bosie!' Ross shouted, 'If this goes to court, Oscar will have to tell lies. Perjure himself. Everything will come out. Whatever the result – it'll be utter disaster.'

'You're an enemy, then!' Bosie challenged.

'No, no – Bosie – please.' This was going too far. He spoke as from a remove, looking from one young man to the other, as if the matters they were discussing concerned someone else and not himself. 'Robbie, you're a dear boy, but I can't even think of leaving the country. As a matter of fact, I can't even leave this hotel.'

Ross stared at him.

'I can't pay the bill,' confessed Oscar. 'Not that that matters. What matters is –'

Ross wasn't having it. 'We can raise you money, for heaven's sake. Anyway, what about your royalties?'

'We shall need all the money we can get for the libel case,' Bosie stated. He was pacing again, becoming even more agitated. 'It's a matter of principle, Robbie. Not something you would understand.'

Ross was furious. He nearly lunged at Bosie, restraining himself only through sheer will power.

'My father can't be allowed to go on making all our lives a torment like this,' said Bosie.

Ross knelt beside Oscar's chair, and pleaded with him in a whisper, 'Oscar, I beg you —'

'I'm not going to run away, Robbie.' Oscar had reached a conclusion that would enable him to do the only thing he possibly could. He suddenly saw a vision of the future in which he played out his destined role. It was not a very reassuring vision, but something of the melancholy he felt at seeing it was pleasant to him.

'I'm not going to hide,' Oscar said. 'That would be the English thing to do.'

'If you take Queensberry to court, all hell will break loose,' replied Ross.

'All my life, I've fought against the English vice.' Oscar paused, allowing this to sink in. The boys stopped, startled. Ross tried to interrupt, but Oscar would have none of it. 'Hypocrisy. Not that that's the point. The point is . . .' There was nothing lofty in his presentation. It was a statement of fact, and an acceptance of his doom. 'Queensberry's already caused the death of one of his sons. If I don't try to stop him now, whom will he harm next?'

Ross looked Oscar, then at Bosie, and he knew that it was hopeless.

Things were not well with Constance back at Tite Street, either. Ross visited frequently and was to some degree a comfort, but certain topics of conversation soon became embarrassing to both of them.

By early March, though, Constance had had enough. She paced the drawing room, walking up and down less as an expression of impatience, and more to ease her painful back. If her physical condition was frail, Constance had nevertheless gained another kind of strength, and Ross was impressed by her clarity and her resolve.

'He hasn't been home since Christmas. He's avoiding me, Robbie.'

'Oh, surely not.'

Constance looked at him. He looked away.

'I know what everyone's saying,' she said, 'but it's not true. Not true . . .' She said this firmly, then stopped and looked at him, questioningly, '. . . is it?'

'Of course not.'

But she didn't really know whether to believe him or not. 'It's so shaming.' Suddenly overcome with back pain, Constance leaned on a chair. Ross jumped to her aid, offering to help her sit.

'No, I find it easier to stand,' she said, waving him off. 'I'm going to Torquay for a month, to try and get my back right. And Oscar's been so busy –'

'I'm sure he'll be terribly upset when he knows you've been in so much pain.'

Waving this aside also, Constance said, 'The truth is, I need some money, and I don't even know where he is to ask for it.'

Ross expressed shock, and Constance continued.

'It does seem rather hard, when he's having such an extraordinary success that I have to ask you to –'

Ross's loyalty was divided. He hesitated for a moment, then said, 'I think I can find him.'

'There isn't going to be trouble, is there? Because if there is, it's not fair to keep me in the dark.'

Ross was silent.

Constance moved to a chair, ready now to sit. Ross helped her down gently.

'I keep hearing these stories about Bosie and his father,' she said.

'I'm sure you don't want to –'

'Yes, I do,' Constance stopped him. 'Men think women should be protected by not knowing. But not knowing only makes it worse. Is there going to be trouble?'

'I – I hope not,' was Ross's rather lame answer. It was the best he could do.

C. O. Humphreys was a bald-headed solicitor of no great acumen. His office was bleak. His style was stilted. What minimal enthusiasm he displayed had more to do with Oscar's celebrity than with the merits of the case.

Oscar seemed unperturbed. Fate was taking its course.

Humphreys responded slowly to Bosie's excited presentation of the situation.

'I believed a prosecution would certainly succeed, provided, and I stress this, provided there is no truth whatever in the accusation made by Lord Queensberry.'

'Of course there's no truth in it!' Bosie blurted.

'Then so long as I have Mr Wilde's assurance that that is indeed the case –'

There was a silence as Humphreys waited uncomfortably for Oscar to respond.

The silence continued.

Then Oscar looked up.

'There is no truth in the accusation whatever.'

'Good,' said Humphreys. Now he was off the hook. 'Excellent. The defence, I understand, will be led by Mr Edward Carson.'

Oscar raised an eyebrow. Another piece had just found its place in the puzzle.

'Old Ned? I was at college with him in Dublin. No doubt he will perform his task with all the added bitterness of an old friend.'

CHAPTER 14

The soul is born old but grows young.
That is the comedy of life. And the
body is born young and grows old.
That is life's tragedy.

THE COURT WAS crowded, not a seat to be had.
A stern sort of judge, Mr Justice Henn Collins, another Irishman educated in Dublin, surveyed the mob with a keen eye, unwilling to stand for theatrics of any kind.

Oscar was dressed in the height of fashion, in a conservative frock coat, with a white flower in his buttonhole. The courtroom, though small, was in a system of discreet boxes and levels. Oscar, located in a middle tier, thought of himself as if in purgatory surrounded by various degrees of angelic and demonic presence not only on all sides, but above and below as well.

He spotted Lord Queensberry, who wore a Cambridge blue hunting stock instead of a collar and tie.

The opening statement for the prosecution was delivered by Sir Edward Clarke, a gifted associate of Humphreys, and all agreed, even the defence, that it was a remarkable forensic achievement and a model of legal strategy, even if Bosie found it too conservative. Clarke was less concerned with overtly attacking Queensberry, and spent most of the statement attempting to prove Oscar's innocence of the libellous attacks made by the Marquess. Anticipating the tactics of the defence, for example, Clarke read the text of an allegedly compromising letter which Queensberry was planning to use in support of his case.

> My own Boy,
>
> Your sonnet is quite lovely, and it is a marvel that those red rose-leaf lips of yours should have been made no less for the music of song than for the madness of kisses. Your slim gilt soul walks between passion and poetry. I know Hyancinthus, whom Apollo loved so madly, was you in Greek days.
>
> Why are you alone in London, and when do you go to Salisbury? Do go there to cool your hands in the grey twilight of Gothic things, and come here whenever you like. It is a lovely place — it only lacks you; but go to Salisbury first.
>
> Always, with undying love,
>
> > Yours,
> > Oscar

'The words of that letter, gentlemen,' observed Clark, 'may appear extravagant to those in the habit of writing commercial correspondence . . .' There was laughter here, 'or those ordinary letters which the necessities of life force upon one every day. But Mr Wilde is a poet, and the letter is considered by him as a prose sonnet, and one of which he is in no way ashamed and is prepared to produce anywhere as the expression of truly poetic feeling, and with no relation whatever to the hateful and repulsive suggestions put to it in the plea in this case.'

Then, after addressing Queensberry's ill-mannered behaviour, Clark went on to justify another key element of the defence's case, 'the volume called *The Picture of Dorian Gray*', concluding with a challenge to the defence. 'I shall be surprised if my learned friend Mr Carson can pitch upon any passage in that book which does more than describe as novelists and dramatists may – nay, must – describe the passions and fashions of life.'

Oscar was pleased. This would be a good act to follow.

Next, Oscar came forth to testify. He stood in the witness box behind a lectern, ready for anything.

Edward Carson – 'Old Ned' as Oscar had called him – was a tall, saturnine man with a rich Irish accent. He cross-examined him with deft thoroughness.

'So far as your works are concerned, you pose as not being concerned about morality or immorality.'

'I don't know what you mean by "pose,"' said Oscar.

'It's a favourite word of yours, is it not?'

'Is it? In writing a play or a book, I am concerned entirely with literature – with art. I do not aim at doing good or evil, but at trying to make a thing that will have some quality of beauty.'

'Listen, sir. Here is one of your pieces of literature – "Wickedness is a myth invented by good people to account for the curious attractiveness of others."'

A ripple of amusement ran through the court.

'You think that true?' asked Carson.

'I rarely think anything I write is true.'

Carson persisted, using yet another quote. ' "If one tells the truth, one is sure, sooner or later, to be found out." '

'That is a pleasing paradox,' said Oscar, 'but I do not set very high store by it as an axiom.'

'Is it good for the young?'

'Anything is good that stimulates thought at whatever age.'

'Whether moral or immoral?'

'There is no such thing as morality or immorality in thought.'

'Well, what about this, then?' asked Carson, reading another passage. ' "Pleasure is the only thing one should live for." '

'I think that the realisation of oneself is the prime aim of life, and to realise through pleasure is finer than to do so through pain. I am, on this point, entirely on the side of the ancients – the Greeks.'

Oscar was completely self-assured, fed by the laughter of his supporters in the gallery. Point for point, he had scored well.

Leaving the court that day, Oscar saw, in a corridor nearby, many of the boys whom he had frequented waiting to give evidence. Among them were Taylor, Wood, Allen and Parker. They were smoking and joking, and all in all it was something of a party for them.

Ross was there as well, anxiously listening to the progress of the trial.

The following day Oscar was less confident. He was not certain why.

In court the subject turned from literature to life.

How long have you known Alfred Taylor?' Carson began.

'About two years, two and a half years.'

'Is he an intimate friend of yours?'

'I would not call him that.'

'But you went often to his rooms.'

'About seven or eight times, perhaps.'

'Did you know Mr Taylor kept ladies' dresses in his rooms?'

'No.'

'Have you ever seen him in ladies' costume?'

'Never.'

By this time, the courtroom had grown very tense. Queensberry was looking pleased. Oscar held his breath.

Carson took a moment to sample the spirit of the room before carrying on.

'Did you know he was notorious for introducing young men to older men?'

'I never heard it in my life.'

'Has he introduced young men to you?'

'Yes.'

'How many young men?'

'About five.'

'And did you call them by their Christian names?'

'Yes.' said Oscar deliberately. 'I always call by their Christians names people whom I like. People I dislike I call something else.'

'Were these young men all about twenty?'

'About that. I like the society of young men.'

'What was their occupation?'

'I really do not know.'

'Well, let me tell you, Mr Wilde,' said Carson, closing in

for the kill. 'There you met a man called Charles Parker, I believe.'

'Yes.'

'Charles Parker is a gentleman's valet.'

Carson let that sink in, looking at the jury. Their faces told all. Oscar's case was in severe jeopardy. It was the social indiscretion, not the sexual allegations, that seemed to turn the tide for them. It made Oscar angry.

'You met his broker there, too, I believe,' Carson continued.

'Yes.'

'He is a groom.'

Again, Carson paused.

'I didn't care twopence what they were,' said Oscar finally. He could taste the anger on his tongue. That, and a profound contempt for those who would judge him. 'I liked them. I have a passion to civilise the community. I recognise no social distinctions at all, of any kind. To me, youth, the mere fact of youth, is so wonderful that I would sooner talk to a young man for half an hour than – well, than be cross-examined in court.'

'Do I understand that even a young boy you might pick up in the street would be a pleasing companion?'

'I would talk to a street Arab with pleasure. If he would talk to me.'

'And take him to your rooms?'

'Yes.'

'And then commit improprieties with him?' Carson shouted this. The question, and the force with which it was thrown into Oscar's face, came out of nowhere.

It rocked Oscar and stunned the courtroom.

'Certainly not,' he replied.

Oscar knew then that he had been trapped.

He took a quick look around the court. The laughter, the smiles and nods of agreement, where gone. He was unsure of what this meant exactly, except that something had gone horribly wrong.

The libel suit would, of course, have to be dropped, Oscar knew that. But the other implications of the course of the trial were still unclear to him.

CHAPTER 15

*Modern journalism, by giving us the
opinions of the uneducated, keeps us in
touch with the ignorance of the
community.*

HUMPHREYS LOOKED VERY grave, and spoke more
gravely still when Oscar visited him later. Against all
rumour to the contrary, he had chosen to believe Oscar's
and Bosie's protestations of innocence.

'You withdraw your libel action against Lord Queensberry – well and good.' Humphreys paced the length of his
office in measured strides, bestowing a kind of authority to
his words. 'But there remains the question of the evidence,
Lord Queensberry's evidence against you. My information
is that the Crown wishes to pursue the matter. In which
case an arrest and a charge of gross indecency are certain to
follow. The maximum sentence is two years' hard labour.'

Oscar had a look of near incomprehension.

Humphreys took a deep breath and continued, even
more deliberately, 'Nine months' hard labour is reckoned
to be more than a man of our –' Humphreys hesitated here,
afraid of giving offence, but also not wishing to be lumped

in the same category of humanity with Oscar, '– our background can survive. My advice to you, Mr Wilde – my advice as a man and as a lawyer, is to take the next train to Paris.'

'B . . . but my children, my boys –' Oscar stuttered, at a complete loss.

'Where are they?'

'Well, they're away, at boarding school. I must go down and see them, I –'

'You have no time for that. In any case, to go and see them now would bring them dreadful ignominy.'

'Ignominy?' Oscar still could not grasp the concept. 'My wife, I must say goodbye to my wife.'

'You have done your wife grievous damage already.'

'Oh, but Constance – I – '

Humphreys was unrelenting. 'Unless you positively wish to subject her to the further humiliation of seeing you arrested and taken away in front of the gutter press, Mr Wilde, you must go.'

That very gutter press was out in force outside the Cadogan Hotel, clamouring to be let in, along with a crowd of eager spectators watching to catch the next sensational development.

Upstairs in his suite, Oscar looked stunned. He put clothes into a suitcase without conviction. He picked up a shirt, then put it down again. Bosie came in with a couple of glasses of hock and seltzer, and handed Oscar one.

Oscar sat in a chair. Ross came up to him and, quietly persuasive, spoke to him.

'Oscar, you must take that train.' Not getting an answer, he tried again. 'Practically everyone you know will be on it.

At least six hundred single gentlemen, all in abject terror of arrest.'

'No. Where your life leads you, you must go.'

Oscar simply could not visualise himself as a fugitive. That would have been the ultimate embarrassment. There was no question to him that suffering would be more becoming. He would somehow carry on, as the great figure, doomed by fate and the unjust laws of a foreign country. There was no dearth in history of writers imprisoned for their integrity. His mind would certainly survive, and he would emerge superior from the indignities heaped upon him. His pain would reveal the hypocrisy of the age and of the nation.

'I'm not ashamed my life has brought me here. One must never deny one's own experience, whatever society may think. I defy society.' Oscar paused and sighed, heavy-hearted. 'But Robbie – dear Robbie, you've always been so – Would you do something for me? Would you tell Constance what's been happening? Why I can't – Would you, Robbie?'

Constance made a show of being very high-spirited and strong when Ross appeared at Tite Street later that afternoon.

'Tell him to go. He must save himself. Tell him to go abroad.'

'We've been telling him all day,' said Ross. 'He won't budge.'

Constance nodded, as if expecting this. 'People have never understood what courage he's needed to be himself. Poor Oscar!'

Ross waited, not knowing how to bring up the subject. Then he said, 'You must go abroad, too.'

Constance took a moment to comprehend this.

Ross elaborated on this theme. 'We must all go abroad. At once.' There was silence from Constance.

Ross persisted, all concern. 'Oscar says – will you tell the boys goodbye?'

She nodded bitterly.

'I need to go through his papers,' he said.

Constance just stared at him.

'I was always too silent,' she said finally. 'If I'd known – Bosie – if I'd only spoken up.'

'It wouldn't have made any difference.'

'Perhaps not. But at least I wouldn't blame myself now.'

Ross went rapidly through Oscar's papers; packing a bag of essentials, removing manuscripts, destroying incriminating letters. He came upon a cache of photographs, pictures of Wood, Taylor and Parker in various stages of undress. He quickly tore them up and put them in the fire.

Then Ross watched from the window as Constance disappeared into a cab.

Later still, and back at the Cadogan Hotel, Bosie and Ross waited for Oscar – trapped in the sitting room – smoking cigarettes, while Speranza, at her most exalted, admonished her son in the bedroom.

'You are an Irish gentleman. Of course you must stay.' Here was an occasion that, with its overtones of social politics and tragedy, was worthy of her and her son.

Oscar looked at her, completely downcast.

'Your father fought when he was libelled,' she rallied. 'I was in the courts myself, I fought.'

'Yes, I know, Madre, but –'

'You will fight these English Philistines and you will win! And even if you lose – even if you go to prison, you will always be my son.'

'Well, it is, of course, too late to change that now,' Oscar said.

The joke fell flat.

'If you go, Oscar, I will never speak to you again.'

'No one will speak to me again whatever I do.' Oscar looked at Speranza, very serious now. 'Of course I'm your son, Madre. Which is why – even if I lose – the English will never forget me.'

From her reaction, from the warmth in her eyes, Oscar knew that what he had said was the affirmation of everything Speranza had ever stood for. He was telling her, in this stiff and political fashion, more characteristic of her than of him, that he loved her, and that he was, indeed, *her* son.

Speranza heard the message, and threw her arms around Oscar.

Moments later, Speranza walked past Bosie and Ross. She moved slowly, bowed down as if by a weight, but with great dignity. Ignoring Bosie completely, she touched Ross's cheek gently as he held the door for her.

In the hallway, just outside the suite, she found a bench and sat on it. Here, in brief solitude, she rested her head on her cane and wept.

Speranza emerged from the hotel into the street and fought

her way through the crowd of reporters, where there was a waiting cab. She held a handkerchief by her face, hoping to avoid detection. It took the reporters only a moment to realise who she was, and in that moment her anger flared. Head held high, handkerchief abandoned, she moved through the crowd like a tornado, bestowing choice epithets on any who stood in her way, her cane a weapon to be feared, her flashing eyes an even greater terror.

As the cab moved off, three of the journalists actually chased after it, with shouts of, 'Lady Wilde! Lady Wilde! Have you anything to say about your son's disgrace?' Their disappointed voices faded to the sound of horses' hooves and wooden wheels on cobblestones.

Oscar was sitting with Ross in his suite at the Cadogan Hotel at ten past six on 5 April, when the knock came. They looked at each other. Moments later came a second, more peremptory knock.

'Come in,' said Ross, standing up.

Two detectives appeared.

'Mr Oscar Wilde, I believe?' asked one of them.

As there was no response from Oscar, it was left to Ross to say impatiently, 'Yes, yes.'

'We have a warrant here for your arrest,' the detective announced, 'on a charge of committing indecent acts.'

At the St James's Theatre, Oscar Wilde's name was blacked out on posters for *The Importance of Being Earnest*. At the Haymarket Theatre, last performance stickers announced the closing of *An Ideal Husband*.

At Tite Street, the blinds were drawn. Paintings were taken down, and sheets covered much of the furniture.

Georgina, Lady Mount-Temple, shared her wisdom of the moment with Constance, while Ada Leverson looked on inscrutably from a doorway, smoking a cigarette.

'I recommend Switzerland,' she advised. 'As soon as possible. No one knows who anyone is in Switzerland and the climate is thoroughly sobering. You will have to change your name, of course.'

'Oh – I can't,' Constance replied softly.

Lady Mount-Temple would not let Constance continue, 'My dear Constance, the name of "Wilde" will be a word of execration for the next thousand years. You can't possibly let your boys grow up with people knowing who they are. Think of their lives at school.'

Although shaken, Constance had had enough.

'Thank you for your advice,' she said with icy politeness. 'I'm sorry our friendship has to end like this.'

In a solicitous tone, Lady Mount-Temple assured her, 'You will always be my friend.'

'I'm still Oscar's wife.'

'That must cease forthwith,' said Lady Mount-Temple severely. 'Forthwith, do you understand? Or you, too, will be cast into outer darkness, as well as your children.' Noting Ada's presence, she went on, 'Anyone who has anything to do with Oscar from now on will never be received in society again. Ever.'

Constance fought her tears, as Ada approached, taking her arm and leading her firmly away from Lady Mount-Temple.

'Oh God, Ada, what's going to happen to him?' Constance said. 'If everyone turns against him –'

Ada stared pointedly at Lady Mount-Temple until she left. Only then did she speak to Constance.

'I've invited him to come and stay with us till the trial is over'.

Ada's kindness was too much for Constance, for she burst suddenly into tears.

CHAPTER 16

*Yes: I am a dreamer. For a dreamer is
one who can only find his way by
moonlight, and his punishment is that
he sees the dawn before the rest of the
world.*

  *Society often forgives the criminal;
it never forgives the dreamer.*

THE SECOND TRIAL began on 26 April 1895 at the Old
Bailey.

Bosie visited Oscar in Holloway Prison, where he was
detained between appearances in court. A long line of
prisoners sat on one side of a metal grille, talking to their
visitors on the other. Officers were everywhere, watching
and listening.

There was a great deal of noise in the room as well, and
Oscar was having ear-trouble, a condition that rendered his
incarceration especially unbearable. Everything around
Oscar contrived to offend; the drabness of the surroundings, the noxious odours, and now the awful noise.

Bosie spoke to him through the grille, having to work

hard to be understood. Oscar was very downcast. Bosie, on the other hand, was very wild.

'Oscar, you must let me go in the witness box,' he said. 'If the jury can only hear what I have to say, how my father has treated my mother –'

'Bosie – darling boy – as soon as they see you in all your golden youth and me in all my – corruption –'

He had never spoken to Bosie of his physical self-disgust before, never even suggested to him that he was less than pleased with his body and its functions. Indeed, he had rarely admitted it to himself.

Bosie's reaction was a violent denial.

'You didn't corrupt me! I corrupted you, if anything!'

'That's not how it will seem.'

'But I must have my say! It's outrageous. Everyone else has said anything that came into his head, but I – I'm the person all this is about! It's me my father wants to get at, not you! It's outrageous that I can't have my say!'

'It won't help, Bosie. It may actually make things worse.'

'But my father will win! I can't endure my father winning!'

And to Oscar it was suddenly perfectly clear that it was against his father and not for Oscar that Bosie wanted, even needed, to give evidence. He was able in this instant to view his life with Bosie in an entirely different light.

'You must go away, dear boy,' said Oscar gently. 'I couldn't bear for them to arrest you.'

'And I can't bear what they're saying about you in court!'

'I couldn't myself, at first. I felt sick with horror. But then I thought how splendid it would have been if I'd been saying all those things about myself.' Bosie opened his eyes

wide in astonishment. Oscar smiled at him and continued.
'It's not the things themselves. It's who says them.'

A bell rang, and the other inmates and their regular
visitors all rose as the end of the session was called.

'Jesus Christ!' Bosie reacted. He seemed ready to attack a
guard. He was not ready to leave.

'Goodbye Bosie, dear boy.'

Oscar grasped Bosie's fingers through the grille and
kissed them.

'Don't let anyone, anything, ever change your feeling for
me, change your love,' Oscar said.

A prison officer called out, 'Time's up, my lord.'

'Oscar, never!' swore Bosie. 'They never will, I won't let
them. I won't let them.'

A second bell rang, and Bosie, slowly and reluctantly,
stood and moved off. At the door, he turned and gave Oscar
a last stare, proud, angry, arrogant and tragically beautiful.
That look was the one Oscar remembered from their
meeting, at the theatre, now so long ago.

Bosie held his eyes for a long moment before disappear-
ing.

Oscar lowered his head.

In court, Queensberry, now wearing a white cravat and a
flower, was present to watch the events unfold with a
characteristic sneer.

Oscar did not wear a flower this time.

He was questioned by Charles Gill for the prosecution.

'You have been a great deal in the company of Lord
Alfred Douglas.'

'Oh, yes.'

'Did he read his poems to you?'

'Yes.'

'So. You can perhaps understand that some of his verses would not be acceptable to a reader with an ordinary balanced mind?'

'I am not prepared to say,' replied Oscar. 'It is a question of taste, temperament and individuality. I should say one man's poetry is another man's poison.'

'Yes, I daresay!' said Gill. 'But in this poem by Lord Alfred Douglas – "Two Loves" – there is one love, "True Love", which, and I quote, "fills the hearts of boy and girl with mutual flame", and there is another – "I am the love that dare not speak its name". Was that poem explained to you?'

'I think it's clear.'

'There is no question as to what it means?'

'Most certainly not.'

'Is it not clear that the love described relates to natural and unnatural love?'

'No.'

'Oh. Then what is the "Love that dare not speak its name"?'

Oscar paused. He looked down, seeking the strength within. He tried to speak, and no sound emerged. Then, he began again.

'The love that dare not speak its name in this century is such a great affection of an elder for a younger man as there was between David and Jonathan, such as Plato made the very basis of his philosophy and such as you may find in the sonnets of Michelangelo and Shakespeare. It is that deep spiritual affection that is as pure as it is perfect. It dictates and pervades great works of art like those of Shakespeare and Michelangelo, and my letters to Lord Alfred, such as they are. It is in this century misunderstood, so much misunderstood that it may be described as "the Love that dare not speak its name", and on account of it I am placed where I am now. It is beautiful, it is fine, it is the noblest form of affection. There is nothing unnatural about it. It is intellectual, and it repeatedly exists between an elder and a younger man, when the elder has intellect, and the younger has all the joy, hope and glamour of life before him. That it should be so, the world does not understand. The world mocks at it and sometimes puts one in the pillory for it.'

A spontaneous outburst of applause rang out from the public gallery; but there were also boos and hisses. The judge, Mr Justice Charles, rapped with his mallet.

'If there is any further manifestation from the public gallery, I will have the court cleared.'

After all the evidence was presented, the jury was removed for deliberations. Four hours later, they sent a communication to the judge that they were 'unable to arrive at an agreement'.

The judge summoned the jury, and observed, 'I am unwilling to do anything at any time which should look like compelling a jury to deliver a verdict. You have been very long in deliberation over this matter, and no doubt you have done your very best to arrive at an agreement on the questions. On the other hand, the inconveniences of another trial are very great and, if you thought there was any prospect of agreement after deliberating further, I would ask you to do so.'

'My lord,' replied the foreman, 'I fear there is no chance of agreement.'

Oscar, waiting in the defendant's box, heard the

announcement that signified a hung jury, and heaved a sigh of relief.

On 7 May, after just over a month in Holloway Prison, Oscar was released on bail.

Three weeks later, on 22 May, he was back at the Old Bailey to stand trial again. This third trial lasted only three days.

On 25 May, the judge, Sir Alfred Wills passed sentence.

'Oscar Wilde, the crime of which you have been convicted is so bad that one has to put stern restraint upon one's self to prevent oneself from describing, in langauge which I would rather not use, the sentiments which must rise in the breast of every man of honour who had heard the details. People who can do these things must be dead to all sense of shame. It is the worst case I have ever tried. I shall pass the severest sentence that the law allows. In my judgement it is totally inadequate for such a case as this. The sentence of the court is that you be imprisoned and held to hard labour for two years.'

Oscar was marched down a corridor. It was crowded on both sides. People jostled to get a view. There was jeering and shouting. Someone spat at him.

One corridor turned into another, and then another, and Oscar's spirits sagged further with each turn. He kept his body upright, and his eyes consciously, even desperately, lighted upon any detail — a face, a window, a corner — which might help him retain a sense of place and time. But very soon only disorientation remained.

By a door, somewhere — he had no idea where —

someone stepped out from the crowd and stood conspicuously apart as Oscar approached. It was Ross. As Oscar was led past, Ross raised his hat in a sign of loyalty. Oscar saw this, and tears came to his eyes. But for a moment he also had a clearer vision not only of where he was, but who he was.

He was marched through the door, then down a long wide circular staircase. When he looked up, he could see Ross in the gallery above, a vision that was to help sustain him in his time of incarceration.

CHAPTER 17

*A slim thing, gold-haired like an
angel, stands always at my side. He
moves in the gloom like a white
flower. I thought but to defend him
from his father. I thought of nothing
else, and now my life seems to have
gone from me. I am caught in a
terrible net. But so long as I think
that he is thinking of me — my sweet
rose, my delicate flower, my lily of
lilies, it is in prison that I shall test
the power of love. I shall see if I can't
make the bitter waters sweet by the
intensity of the love I bear you. None
of God's created beings, and you are
the Morning Star to me, have been so
wildly worshipped, so madly adored.*

OSCAR WAS ALONE in his comfortless cell. He became a
wreck, a mere shell of what he had been. He worked a
treadmill alongside the other prisoners, its cold, mechanical

whine an almost ever-present reminder, just at the edge of conscious hearing, of where he was. In the exercise yard, with the other prisoners, he trudged around daily. They wore hoods to inhibit recognition and discourage conversation.

He saw children, prisoners of eleven and twelve, picking hemp until their small hands bled, under the watchful eyes of warders.

Each day became more difficult for him. He stumbled on the treadmill, nearly fell into the works. No sympathy there.

His clothes itched. His eyes burned. What remained of his high aesthetic was translated into an habitual, obsessive handling of the few props allowed him. A plate, a cup, a spoon would be rearranged again and again, so that they lined up just so. They never seemed quite right until he had moved them about and stared at them and moved them about again. It became a compulsion that possessed him. As his hands took to shaking, it became harder to accomplish the necessary right angles and parallels, and it took him longer and longer to perform the task.

In time he lost his strength to the point of requiring assistance to move about.

In Italy, far from any prying eyes that might know them, Bosie and Ross were perched on a terrace overlooking a courtyard, and beyond that, the mountains and the sea. Ross sported the disguise of a fine full moustache, and sipped wine defensively, while Bosie, looking a trifle older and feeling very sorry for himself, paced about.

'Someone's been working on him against me,' said Bosie. 'Saying I must give him back his letters and his presents. But I'm not giving anything back. Not if they make me stay abroad to the end of my life. Oscar is mine. He knows it, I know it. I won't give him up or anything he gave me.'

'That's very – honourable, Bosie, but –'

'It's got nothing to do with honour. I've sworn undying love.' Bosie paused, thinking himself very noble, actually. 'With me, undying means undying. He asked me never to change. Those were his last words to me, not to change.'

'His life will have to change when he comes out. He'll have no money at all.'

Bosie sat.

'What are you insinuating?'

'I'm not insinuating anything,' said Ross quietly. 'I'm just saying, he won't be able to afford anything like the life you and he –'

'Oh, so you're blaming me, too, now are you!'

'I'm not blaming anyone. Bosie, you're not the only person on earth Oscar cares about.'

'You've always hated me, Robbie!' said Bosie petulantly. 'Because Oscar loved and still loves me, when you were never more than one of his boys! I'm suffering just as much as he is, you know!'

Ross doubted this very much, but didn't say so. Bosie continued undaunted, 'My life's ruined, too. And I'm much younger than he is. I've hardly had any life, and it's ruined already. When Oscar gets out, we'll live together properly, whatever you or anyone else says. We'll take a villa somewhere, near here, Posillipo or Ischia –'.

'Or Capri,' said Ross sarcastically.

Bosie, for once, did not rise to the bait. 'I'll take care of him, and give him everything he wants.'

Ross's opinion of this obvious fantasy showed on his face, but Bosie went on like a spoiled child.

'Oscar's mine! And I'm going to have him!'

He jumped up and marched off.

Ross did not attempt to follow.

A waiter brought the bill.

Ross paid.

Years went over, and the Giant grew very old and feeble. He could not play about any more, so he sat in a huge armchair — and watched the children at their games, and admired his garden. 'I have many beautiful flowers,' he said, 'but the children are the most beautiful flowers of all.'

When Constance came to visit Oscar, she saw someone very different from the man she had known. The grey, coarse fabric of his prison suit looked as if it itched unbearably. His face had a sickly pastiness about it, and his eyes were puffy and rimmed in red. His hair, once such a source of pride with him, was unevenly shorn, so that a few spikes pointed this way and that. She was shocked.

Oscar was shocked as well, seeing himself, as if for the first time, in her eyes. And then shocked again at her news.

'Cyril and Vyvyan . . . *Holland*,' he intoned. What was this *Holland*? A name? There was information here that he was not at first able to grasp.

'We were at a hotel in Switzerland,' explained Constance, painfully, 'where – when they found out who we were, they asked us to leave . . .'

There was a silence as Oscar registered the horror of what he'd done to her and his children.

'They – the boys are well?'

'Very well, really. Cyril − I'm afraid Cyril has got some sort of idea of what − of why you're here.' Constance tried to help by being very reasonable and practical, 'I'm sending them to school in Germany, but . . .' she stretched, feeling the pain in her back. 'I can't manage them on my own.'

'Your back isn't any better, then?'

'No, not really. I may have to have an operation.'

Oscar took another moment, gathering his strength for what he needed to say to her, then began, in a halting fashion, 'What I've done to you and the boys − I can't − I shall never forgive myself.' He looked to her for help. 'If we could choose our natures. If we could only choose. You can't imagine how − in here − how I've wished − I've wished a thousand things. But it's no use. Whatever our natures are, we must fulfil them. Or, our lives − my life − would have been filled with dishonesty . . . with more dishonesty than it was.' Oscar looked up at Constance again. 'I have always loved you, Constance. You must believe me.'

There was nothing left for Constance but the truth.

'I don't see how you can have done. Not truly. Not if, all the time −'

'I didn't know,' said Oscar.

She looked him in the eyes as he gestured helplessly, trying desperately to be understood, 'Know thyself, I used to say. And I didn't know myself. I didn't know.' Almost brightening, Oscar changed the subject to more practical matters, putting a brave face on it all. 'I suppose you want a divorce,' he said, asking a question to which he felt he already knew the answer. 'You have every reason.'

Constance did not respond directly. She coughed lightly.

'I've been thinking,' she said, 'when you do come out, when they let you out, you can come to Switzerland or

Italy, write another play, get yourself back –' Oscar shook his head. 'You can. You're so clever, you can –'

'Everything I've ever written, I've written for England,' said Oscar firmly. 'England has taken everything away from me.'

'You're Irish.'

He said nothing. Her heart melted.

'Oscar, I don't want a divorce.'

Unbelievable, and yet true. He had hoped against hope. There was yet one other crucial question. He began to sob as he asked it. 'Will you ever let me see the children again?'

'Of course,' said Constance, and she saw the joy that this gave him. 'But there must be one condition. Oscar, you must never see Bosie again.' Her tone was firm and uncompromising. Her eyes grew momentarily cold, colder than he had ever thought possible.

Oscar looked at her through his tears. He remembered seeing her like this once before, not a face so much as a stained-glass composite in hues of light muddled by the tears.

'If I saw Bosie now, I'd kill him.' This was true. Looking at Constance at this moment, he knew it, and he felt it passionately.

A tiny, almost unnoticeable smile crossed Constance's features. It looked to Oscar like a smile of triumph, but he didn't really care.

'The children love you, Oscar.' Constance reached out and took his hand firmly in hers. 'They'll always love you.'

Oscar's hand trembled as he held on to hers as if it were a lifeline.

'Did anyone tell you?' she said. 'They've been perform-ing *Salome* in Paris.'

There was no response from Oscar. He'd wanted so much to get the play produced, and now it seemed to mean so little.

When Constance had left, Oscar nearly collapsed, shedding what illusory strength he had mustered for her visit. He allowed a prison guard to lead him back to his cell. He leaned even more heavily than usual upon his helper.

CHAPTER 18

> *The Giant hastened across the grass,*
> *and came near to the child. And when*
> *he came quite close his face grew red*
> *with anger, and he said, 'Who hath*
> *dared to wound thee?' For on the*
> *palms of the child's hands were the*
> *prints of two nails, and the prints of*
> *two nails were on the little feet.*

OSCAR HAD BEEN given paper, and was now allowed to write. It was perhaps the only thing that kept him sane.

A warder entered the cell.

'That's enough for today,' he said.

'Oh, but I was –'

'Come on, you know the rules.'

Oscar bundled the pieces of paper together and gave them to the warder, who left with them.

Then Oscar walked the very few steps to his barred window and gazed at his small square of sky.

'Who hath dared to wound thee?' cried the Giant; 'tell me, that I

may take my big sword and slay him.' 'Nay!' answered the child: 'but these are the wounds of Love.'

'Who art thou?' said the Giant, and a strange awe fell on him, and he knelt before the little child. And the child smiled on the giant, and said to him, 'You let me play once in your garden, to-day you shall come with me to my garden, which is Paradise.' And when the children ran in that afternoon, they found the Giant lying dead under the tree, all covered with white blossoms.

Ross and Ada met in the sitting room of a hotel. They sat in a private booth in a quiet corner, having tea. He described his last meeting with Bosie, still incredulous at the man's arrogance.

'Bosie thinks I'm jealous.'

Ada simply touched his arm.

'I think it will come as a shock to Bosie to realise that even he is unimportant in the scheme of things.' She sighed. 'But no doubt Bosie will be remembered as long as Oscar . . . unfortunately.'

'How long will that be?' asked Ross.

'As long as people want to laugh – then wonder why they're laughing. Oscar has always been a legend, and now he's a fact. The great moralists are always punished, but at least it makes them famous. Socrates, Jesus –'

Ross looked shocked.

'I'm sorry,' said Ada. 'I always forget you're a believer. Perhaps I'm surprised that you still are, seeing how Oscar's changed the way we all think.'

'Perhaps I'm not strong enough to think like him.' Ross was very serious about this, his tone was confessional. 'I sometimes wonder, if I hadn't – pushed him – into –'

'Don't,' said Ada. 'Oscar was lucky to meet you, Robbie. Think who else it might have been.'

Ross nodded in gratitude, knowing that she was right.

'Must you go abroad again at once?' she asked.

'I shouldn't be here now.'

'But . . . has he got anywhere to go when he is released?'

'It'll have to be France. I'm going to see what I can arrange.'

'But here – when he leaves prison?'

On the morning of 18 May 1897, Oscar emerged from Pentonville Prison, carrying a suitcase and a large envelope.

Ada, wearing a smart hat, waited for him with a cab. She said nothing about Oscar's appearance, but stood there, looking at him kindly, letting him take his time.

'My dear Sphinx,' he said, kissing her warmly on both cheeks, 'how marvellous of you to know what hat to wear at seven in the morning to meet a friend who has been away!'

The cabman took the suitcase, and reached for the envelope, but Oscar waved him off, saying, 'Thank you. I'll take care of this.'

Ada eyed him curiously, 'What is it?'

'It's a letter to Bosie, explaining why I shall love him for ever but never see him again. I want Robbie to get it copied before I send it. I rather think Bosie may throw it in the fire. I call it *De Profundis*. It comes from the very depths.'

Oscar looked about him and saw the day, and a joy that could never be taken away mounted in his heart.

They got in, and the cab rolled away.

On a stormy evening at Berneval Beach in France, the waves

crashing down, Oscar, wrapped in a cloak, walked along the deserted front.

He recited a poem, his last.

> 'I know not whether Laws be right,
>   Or whether Laws be wrong;
> All that we know who lie in gaol
>   Is that the wall is strong;
> And that each day is like a year,
>   A year whose days are long.

Another figure emerged from out of the gloom, and Ross was at his side.

One day in the summer of 1898, Oscar walked through a cemetery at the foot of the hills near Genoa. He wore a black suit and a broad-brimmed hat.

He approached a headstone, knelt down beside it, and lay a posy of flowers on the grave.

The inscription read 'Constance Mary, daughter of Horace Lloyd, QC'. He felt momentarily as if he had never existed.

Constance had died in April as the result of an unsuccessful operation on her spine. She had been forty.

> Yet each man kills the thing he loves,
>   By each let this be heard,
> Some do it with a bitter look,
>   Some with a flattering word.
> The coward does it with a kiss,
>   The brave man with a sword!

Some kill their love when they are young,
*   And some when they are old;*
Some strangle with the hands of Lust,
*   Some with the hands of Gold.*
The kindest use the knife, because
*   The dead so soon grow cold.*

And in a French café, still later that year, Oscar sat with Ross
at an outdoor table, drinking red wine.

Ross had read *The Ballad of Reading Gaol*. He was tremen-
dously moved by the poem, and insisted that Oscar should
continue writing.

'I'm sure we can find a hotel near here . . . so that way
you can work.'

Oscar stared at his plate. He gathered the silverware, and
moved knife, fork and spoons into parallels around his
plate. Unhappy with the way they lined up, he continued
moving them about.

Ross reached out across the table, and gently touched his
hands.

Oscar stopped, then looked directly at Ross.

'I've decided to see him, Robbie.'

'Yes . . . well. I thought you had.'

'I can't live without love. I have nothing else left. I've
lost my wife, I've lost my children – they won't allow me
to see them now. No one will ever read my plays or books
again . . .'

'Of course they will!' cried Ross.

'The *Ballad* is my swansong.' Oscar thought for a
moment. 'I could live with you, Robbie – yes, easily, and so
much better. But you – you have other calls, and Bosie –'
Oscar paused unhappily. 'My life has always been romantic,

and for better, or usually worse, Bosie is my romance. A tragedy, as well. But a romance none the less. He loves me.'

Ross started to say something, but Oscar cut him off.

'He loves me more than he loves anyone else. As much as he can love. And allow himself to be loved.'

Ross smiled. 'I think we need some more wine.' He poured them each a fresh glass, remembering, 'I find that alcohol, when taken in sufficient quantity . . .'

'. . . can bring about all the effects of drunkenness.' Oscar finished the thought, letting the wine, and the afternoon sun and Ross's smile warm him.

Most people live for love and admiration. But it is by love and admiration that we should live. If any love is shown us we should recognise that we are quite unworthy of it.

In a colonnaded piazza high on an ancient Italian wall, a small lizard basked and blinked, barely visible amidst the chiaroscuro effect of reflected sunlight on warm stone.

A carriage arrived, sending a brief dust devil into the pastel air.

Porters rushed forth from the small hotel to attend to the mounds of luggage the new arrival had brought.

Bosie descended from the vehicle, as young and beautiful as ever. He looked around, and spotted Oscar, standing just back from view in the shadows of the pillars. Bosie grinned, a rare and powerfully impish grin, and called to him.

As the dust settled on stone and fountain and lizard, Oscar stepped out of the shadows and raised his hat, then moved slowly, almost unwillingly, towards the waiting Bosie.

Life cheats us with shadows. We ask it for pleasure. It gives it to us, with bitterness and disappointment in its train. And we find ourselves looking with a dull heart of stone at the tress of gold-flecked hair that we had once so wildly worshipped and so madly kissed.

In this world there are only two tragedies. One is not getting what one wants. The other is getting it.

Oscar and Bosie parted after three months.

Imprisonment had ruined Oscar's health. He spent his last days in Paris, living in a cheap hotel. He wrote, 'Like dear St Francis of Assisi I am wedded to poverty, but in my case the marriage is not a success.'

Oscar Wilde died on 30 November 1900, aged 46.

Bosie died in 1945.

Robbie Ross died in 1918. In 1950 his ashes were placed in Oscar's tomb.

Wilde

PRODUCTION INFORMATION

In recent times, the literary reputation of Oscar Wilde has shaken itself free of the cloak of scandal which had enveloped it since his trial and imprisonment a hundred years ago. Social and academic attitudes have changed and Wilde is now properly established as one of the most important figures in British literary history.

At last, at the end of the 20th century, it is possible for a film to present a rounded picture of the Irish-born writer, of his hubris and of the consuming passion which brought him down. No longer is there any need to falsify or ignore the sexual elements which are important parts of this story; equally, the importance of Wilde's wife and children to him and, above all, the crucial importance of his work, can all be examined without the need to weight one part against the other. All play a central role in the life of this most complex of geniuses.

Wilde stars Stephen Fry, Jude Law, Vanessa Redgrave, Jennifer Ehle, Gemma Jones, Judy Parfitt, Michael Sheen, Zoë Wanamaker and Tom Wilkinson. Directed by Brian Gilbert from an original screenplay by Julian Mitchell, based on 'Oscar Wilde' by Richard Ellmann, *Wilde* is produced by Marc Samuelson and Peter Samuelson. Michiyo Yoshizaki, Michael Viner, Deborah Raffin, Alan Howden and Alex Graham are executive producers and the line producer is Nick O'Hagan. The production designer is Maria Djurkovic, costume designer Nic Ede, director of photography Martin Fuhrer, editor Michael Bradsell, sound recordist Jim Green-horn, casting director Sarah Bird and the music is composed and conducted by Debbie Wiseman. Make-up is by Pat Hay, the wigs are designed by Stephen Rose, location managers are Rachel Neale and Amanda Stevens and the first assistant director is Cordelia Hardy.

Wilde is a Samuelson Production in association with Dove International Inc, NDF International Ltd/Pony Canyon Inc, Pandora Film, Capitol Films and BBC films, with the participation of the Greenlight Fund. UK theatrical and video rights are with PolyGram Filmed Entertainment and UK pay-TV rights are with BSkyB.

THE FILM STORY

In 1883, Irish-born Oscar Wilde returned to London bursting with exuberance from a year long lecture tour of the United States and Canada. Full of talent, passion and, most of all, full of himself, he courted and married the beautiful Constance Lloyd.

A few years later, Wilde's wit, flamboyance and creative genius were widely renowned. His literary career had achieved notoriety with the publication of *The Picture of Dorian Gray*. Oscar and Constance now had two sons whom they both loved very much. But one evening, Robert Ross, a young Canadian house guest, seduced Oscar and forced him finally to confront the homosexual feelings that had gripped him since his schooldays.

Oscar's work thrived on the realisation that he was gay, but his private life flew increasingly in the face of the decidedly anti-homosexual conventions of late Victorian society. As his literary career flourished, the risk of a huge scandal grew ever larger.

In 1892, on the first night of his acclaimed play *Lady Windermere's Fan*, Oscar was re-introduced to a handsome young Oxford undergraduate, Lord Alfred Douglas, nick-named 'Bosie'. Oscar was mesmerised by the cocky, dashing and intelligent young man and began the passionate and stormy relationship which consumed and ultimately destroyed him.

While Oscar had eyes only for Bosie, he embraced the promiscuous world that excited his lover, enjoying the company of rent boys. In following the capricious and amoral Bosie, Oscar neglected his wife and children, and suffered great guilt. And then the dragon awoke. Bosie's father, the violent, eccentric, cantankerous Marquess of Queensberry, became aware that Bosie, whose 'unmanly' and careless behaviour he despised, was cavorting around London with its greatest playwright, Oscar Wilde.

In 1895, days after the triumphant first night of *The Importance of Being Earnest*, Queensberry stormed into Wilde's club, The Albemarle, and finding him absent left a card with the porter, addressed 'To Oscar Wilde posing Somdomite' (misspelling the insult). Bosie, who hated his father, persuaded Oscar to sue the Marquess for libel. As homosexuality was itself illegal, Queensberry was able to destroy Oscar's case at the trial by calling as witnesses rent boys who would describe Wilde's sexual encounters in open court.

Oscar lost the libel case against Queensberry and was arrested by the crown. With essentially no credible defence against charges of homosexual conduct, he was convicted and sentenced to two years hard labour, the latter part in Reading Gaol. Unreformed Dickensian prison conditions caused a calamitous series of illnesses and brought him to death's door.

Constance fled the country with their children and changed the family name, always hoping that Oscar would return to his family and give up Bosie, now also living in exile.

When Oscar was released from prison in 1897, he tried to comply with Constance's wishes, sending Bosie a deeply moving epic letter, *De Profundis*, explaining why he could never see him again. Following Constance's death in Italy, love, passion, obsession and loneliness combined, however, to defeat prudence and discretion. Despite the certain knowledge that their relationship was doomed, Oscar was unable to resist temptation and he and Bosie were reunited, with disastrous consequences.

'In this world there are only two tragedies. One is not getting what one wants, and the other is getting it.' – Oscar Wilde

ABOUT THE PRODUCTION

Wilde started production at the end of August 1996. The nine-and-a-half week schedule took in a variety of locations, from the grand surroundings of London's Athenaeum Club and Somerset House, to the Victorian splendour of Swanage Pier and the leafy banks of the River Cherwell in Oxford. Key scenes were filmed at stately Knebworth and Luton Hoo and in the forbidding confines of the recently-vacated Oxford Prison. Grip House Studios near London housed the prison treadmill and the interior of a Colorado silver mine, the exterior of which was re-created in the mountains near Alicante. The production's flying visit to Spain also included filming in Granada, which hosted scenes set in a French café and an Italian cemetery.

The film re-teams director Brian Gilbert with producers Marc Samuelson and Peter Samuelson, following their collaboration on the critically-acclaimed *Tom & Viv*, which garnered four Academy Award nominations, two for Oscars and two for BAFTAs. The screenplay is by Julian Mitchell (*Another Country, August*) and is based on the late Richard Ellmann's definitive biography of Oscar Wilde.

Actor-writer Stephen Fry (*Peter's Friends, Cold Comfort Farm*) portrays Wilde, with rising star Jude Law (*Shopping, Gattaca*) as his lover Bosie. Academy award-winner Vanessa Redgrave (*Julia*, *Howard's End*) stars as Oscar's mother Speranza, with Jennifer Ehle (*Pride and Prejudice*, *Paradise Road*), as the playwright's wife, Constance. Gemma Jones (*Sense and Sensibility*, *Feast of July*) is Lady Queensberry, Judy Parfitt (*Maurice*, *Dolores Claiborne*) is the formidable Lady Mount-Temple, Michael Sheen (*Mary Reilly*, *Othello*) is Oscar's first love Robbie Ross, Zoë Wanamaker (*The Hunger*, *Love Hurts*) plays Oscar's acerbic friend Ada Leverson and Tom Wilkinson (*In The Name of The Father*, *The Ghost and the Darkness*) stars as Wilde's nemesis, The Marquess of Queensberry.

The behind-the-camera talent includes Swiss-born, Cable Ace Award winning director of photography Martin Fuhrer (*Tom & Viv*, *Lord of The Flies*), production designer Maria Djurkovic (*The Young Poisoner's Handbook*), costume designer Nic Ede (*Not Without My Daughter*, *Loch Ness*), make-up designer Pat Hay (*White Mischief*, *Richard III*), editor Michael Bradsell (*Henry V*, *Victory*) and award winning composer Debbie Wiseman (*Tom & Viv*).

BRINGING *WILDE* TO
THE SCREEN

Following the success of their collaboration on Tom & Viv,
producers Marc and Peter Samuelson and director Brian
Gilbert were looking for a suitable project with which to
continue their association. Some years earlier, Gilbert had
unsuccessfully pursued the rights to Richard Ellmann's
acclaimed biography of Oscar Wilde. The Samuelsons
managed to secure these book rights and the services of
screenwriter Julian Mitchell and, after almost two years in
development, *Wilde* was ready for the screen.

'When I was asked to do it, my initial reaction was,
Fantastic!' says Mitchell. 'He's such a major figure and I
hadn't really thought about him for about 20 or 30 years,
so it was a wonderful chance to read everything again. The
really good thing about Wilde – why he is internationally
so widely-known – is that his remarks aren't just funny,
they are deeply thought-provoking. They are very subver-
sive of conventional ideas and conventional behaviour.'

Stephen Fry endorses Mitchell's enthusiasm: 'One of the
things I love Oscar for is his denial of convention, his sense
of paradox, his hedonistic refusal to believe anything which
wasn't tested by experience – taking nothing on trust.

There's something about him, the more one learns about him, that appeals to everybody.'

'Oscar Wilde is a world phenomenon,' agrees Mitchell, 'and for many good reasons. The Importance of Being Earnest is one of the best comedies ever written in English and his lines have never been forgotten – everybody knows them.

'I saw the recent London production of An Ideal Husband and there was a 100-year-old play about hypocrisy and sexuality which mirrors the history of Britain in the last 15 years – a series of sexual and financial scandals involving politicians. British political life never changes and Wilde is very acute about it – he's a wonderfully intelligent, accessible man which explains his huge popularity. He isn't a joker – he's not capering around in a funny hat, though he wears wonderful clothes . . . he has terrific style. For him, style was a moral attitude and I think people really respond to that. I'm sure he worked at his epigrams and aphorisms in his study, but he also had a great natural wit and was able to throw off very funny remarks all the time. But when he was being serious he was very serious. The Soul of Man Under Socialism and The Critic as Artist are both profound examinations of late-Victorian society, which have a lot to say to us still.'

Stephen Fry has been an admirer of Wilde since his schooldays. 'He had a phenomenal mind. One of the things he could do was read a novel very, very fast – unbelievably fast. He used to be able to read a book in 20 minutes and tell you the plot and then he could recite huge passages from a novel the size of Middlemarch.

'He read in German, Italian, French and Russian. He really had a quite extraordinary mind, he had read more than anybody else. He was an extraordinary critic because nothing passed him by, he knew popular culture as well as anybody. At the time he was taken for a poseur but he was a great literary mind, a philosopher and a wonderful political essayist.

'It's interesting to realise that Wilde lived in Victorian London at exactly the same time as Sherlock Holmes was supposed to have done. When he met Conan Doyle, Doyle remarked what a great conversationalist Oscar was. It was then pointed out that Wilde had only got in a couple of sentences and Doyle had done all the talking! But that was the point about Wilde, he was a great listener, not somebody who dominated. He made everybody around the room feel more intelligent for being there and he didn't weigh them down with the speed of his mind. He opened his mind to things around him. He had the very rare blend of a faultless verbal ear and a beautiful colour sense – they don't usually go together. When he toured America he gave lectures on interior decoration.'

FAMILY VALUES

One of the key elements in the portrayal of Wilde on screen is a side of his character that is often overlooked – his devotion to his wife, Constance and his sons Cyril and Vyvyan. In Vyvyan Holland's book *Son of Oscar Wilde*, he describes his father as being enchanting, mending his son's toys and telling them stories.

Oscar's marriage to Constance was extremely important to him. According to Julian Mitchell, 'the story of their relationship is something which I think would have to have been made very black-and-white in the old days. Now we can show far more of the shades. She's a very sympathetic character and she did her best to behave very, very well, although hundreds of people around her were telling her she should just cut him off.

'I think that one forgets how much of a male society it was. The sexes were much more separate than today. Oscar used to tell Constance what she should wear. He sort of invented her – he got her involved in dress reform and in various women's organisations. But it was a very male society – a sort of club society – and when men went off together, nobody took much notice. You had given your wife two kids – what more could she ask? And in the upper classes all you had to do, if you were a woman, was to give your husband two legitimate male children.'

Jennifer Ehle admires the woman she plays: 'I think that Constance's story bears testament to her strength of character – her strength as a person. She refused to run for cover when things got rough and she showed great patience, forebearance and loyalty during the times when Oscar started to spend more and more time away.

'She had great belief in him. He had some prospects when they married, but in no way was his future assured. But she believed in him and I think she believed him to be a genius. I do think there was something in her that wanted to attach herself to somebody that she cold almost live vicariously through. As a woman in those days you couldn't stand on your own and be successful. To have a successful husband was quite a wonderful and valid ambition. She was very, very bright and loved Oscar a great deal.'

But wasn't he famously homosexual? 'In our approach to the film we have to make our own choices as to how much she may have suspected or known about homosexuality, let alone suspecting her husband of practising it. It was no different to her than having a suspicion that he was seeing another woman, but when the horror of the truth hit, she was very brave.'

'How much Constance knew and how much she wanted to know really isn't clear,' says Mitchell. 'To me, the really scandalous thing is that Robbie Ross seduced Wilde in his own house when Constance was being extremely nice to him. That was a monstrous breach of good manners!'

Stephen Fry hopes that people will gain a sense of Oscar's kindness and generosity from the film, as well as the importance to him of his family, despite his apparent neglect of them. 'Yes, he did that, in the same way that in a heterosexual marriage people abandon their wives. They adulterise, but it doesn't mean that they don't love their wife and children. He didn't abandon them in the sense of leaving them, he was imprisoned. His wife died and her relatives insisted through a lawyer that he wouldn't be allowed to see his children again. And that was the single thing that broke his heart in the whole catastrophe.

'He didn't abandon them in any real sense, except that of the betrayal of adultery that goes on every day. We all have friends who have not been honest to their wives or husbands. We don't damn them to the inner circle of Hell for it, we understand that people do that. It's perfectly possible to have an affair with another woman or another man and still to love your children.

'Oscar was not a professional homosexual – the word didn't even exist until André Gide started using it as a noun rather than an adjective – and Oscar's love for his wife and children was absolute. To some that may seem rather odd – ''people should be seen to be either one thing or the other'' – but the film takes a more complex and realistic view.'

HOMOSEXUALITY AND SOCIETY

For all the constraints of the Victorian period, men could in some respects be freer than in recent history in their attitudes and behaviour to one another. As director Brian Gilbert describes it: 'Men could be much more affectionate and could be seen to be more affectionate, without causing suspicion or innuendo. So much so, that even many of Oscar's friends did not believe that he was homosexual until he actually told them that he was. It was an interesting cultural question whether, before the Wilde scandal, there was any notion at all of a 'gay man'. There was a very strong sense of what constituted sin, and this was exhaustive and, as it were, intellectually sufficient, requiring no further elaboration: fornication was a sin, adultery was a sin, sodomy was a sin – so indeed was breach of promise to a fiancée. To commit the act of sodomy reflected on an individual's morals, but did not imply a psychological profile. That is to say that there was not yet a gay stereotype, that of 'the homosexual' who because of his sexuality had certain definable characteristics, dispositions, and tastes.

'No doubt, it was around Wilde's time that such stereotyping was beginning – the psycho-analytic movement was in its earliest stages – but it was the Wilde scandal itself that helped crystallise the stereotype. Everything about Wilde himself – his wit, his poise, his love of beauty, poetry, fondness for interior decoration, etc., etc., could now play as evidence of his so-called vice. Such tastes in future lost their innocence and could be freighted with darker implications. Later, during the twenties, that became very fixed in the British public's mind, because many of the Oxbridge generation of the twenties, gay and straight, modelled themselves on Wilde, partly in order to scandalise their parents, but also in reaction against the universally acknowledged heroism of their elders who had fallen in battle and with which it was impossible for them to compete. Thereafter the "Oxford manner", affected by many Oxford men right up to the fifties, had something of Wilde about it.'

Nonetheless, the notion of Oscar Wilde as a prominent gay personality of the period is central to the film. Says Gilbert, 'I suppose anybody who has any ideas about homosexuality has to confront Oscar Wilde. He represents the great challenge to all preconceptions and prejudice. You can't get round him. I think that's wonderful. He is also rare among artists of genius in that he was also an immensely decent and kindhearted man. I do think though, that, while on the surface we have become much more liberal and progressive, underneath it's still seen as a huge threat to society. We're relatively open-minded and tolerant, but unconventional sexual behaviour can be a problem for even the most well-intended and fair-minded people.

'I couldn't say we are simply blaming Victorian hypocrisy and all the rest. In a way that's not the issue. I don't think the Victorians were more hypocritical than we are. Yes, society is to blame in the larger sense. At that time it was profoundly intolerant for other reasons. Historians have debated the influence of the Empire – this great effort that was at its peak during Wilde's time – and we do refer to this in the film. Almost every middle class or upper class family had somebody out in India or in the Colonies somewhere. To the British the harsh facts of colonialism were disguised by the dream of empire – a tremendous and extraordinary fantasy – and a great deal of knowledge of what their men got up to when they were away was simply repressed, or benignly re-interpreted.

'The British ruling class at that time was for a brief period more homogeneous than it had ever been. For about fifty years they all went to public schools, all went to the major universities, they went to clubs, they married late, they were bachelors for a long time. There was a great deal of homosexual activity at public school, much more than there is now because the boys had much less adult supervision within the boarding houses. To that extent there was quite serious hypocrisy amongst people then about Oscar Wilde, because at school you could not avoid seeing homosexual acts. Many of the men who became eminent participated at school, even if they rejected it later and, because there was no fixed idea of being a homosexual, it was simply one other thing that they felt guilty about.'

Very little detail is actually known of Wilde's secret life, as Fry confirms: 'Nobody's quite sure of his physical involvement in his affairs. There is strong evidence to suppose he had some element of physical self-disgust. He worshipped the idea of youth – it was not pederastic or anything – but he felt that young people had the right experience to judge his work. The moments of sexual activity in the film are not to sensationalise it at all – it's rather poignant and affectionate.'

Julian Mitchell agrees that the physical side of Oscar's relationships should be a part of the film. 'It would be dishonest not to show it, the seduction and the physical passion. If you remove the physical passion from the relationship, you're leaving out something essential. People who "come out" late in life as Oscar did, in his late thirties, often lose all sense of balance and I think that's what happened to him. Oscar was overwhelmed by Lord Alfred Douglas. Bosie is a tragic character really but, unfortunately, he's a terribly destructive one. It is actually one of the great love stories – the destruction of this wonderful man by a tortured youth.'

Brian Gilbert does not apportion blame, 'although some of the audience will feel really aggrieved that Bosie had such a hold over Wilde. But we do try to be very candid about the relationship. It's like a marriage – there are certain licences and liberties within a relationship which you cannot judge very easily from the outside. One of the partners might be aggressive, but often has been given permission to be aggressive by the passive one. There are things that are very difficult to judge – it's fascinating dramatic material – but we don't blame Bosie.'

Fry agrees: 'Bosie, according to his own lights, was behaving that way for all the right reasons. His real tragedy was that he was so like his father – they were very, very similar – and, though he did love Oscar, his bad behaviour came from hatred of his father. In a film you see what you would never have seen in life. There are no hidden cameras in a relationship and we don't know how Oscar behaved on his own. We must believe that when Oscar and Bosie found themselves together, they found something in each other which was really valuable – and that was real love, full of passion and madness.'

WILDE THE OUTSIDER

Oscar Wilde was never truly assimilated into London society and, shunned for his homosexuality, remained an outsider until his death. Initially, it was his Irishness that set him apart. His father was a distinguished Dublin surgeon and a man of wide scientific interest, including natural history, ethnology and Irish antiquarian topography, who had been knighted by Queen Victoria. But when Oscar Fingal O'Flahertie Wills Wilde moved to London, followed shortly by his widowed mother and his brother Willie, he found that many people in the city were uncomfortable with his non-Englishness, his flamboyant style and his willingness to challenge the status quo.

Lady Wilde was an enormous influence on Oscar, as producer Marc Samuelson attests: 'She was a very flamboyant society figure who was also a major Irish revolutionary leader and a fairly significant poet as well, who used to write under the name of Speranza. After Sir William Wilde died she came to London in very straitened circumstances, but she and Oscar were incredibly close and she played a significant role in his life.

'In a sense she was overpowering; there's a great quote about Oscar and Bosie – "the over-loved meets the under-loved" – and Oscar did have this incredibly powerful relationship with his mother. After he lost the libel case, a lot of his friends were telling him to flee the country. Speranza famously said, "If you stay, even if you go to prison, you will always be my son. But if you go, I will never speak to you again."'

Julian Mitchell also acknowledges her importance to Oscar's story: 'The real influences on his life are his mother, Bosie and Robbie Ross. Being Irish, being homosexual, at that period meant being an outsider, an observer of society – and, of course, he was a parvenu. One of the cruellest things Bosie used to say about him was that he's always writing about the upper classes, but doesn't really know what they're like. He uses them in the way that any artist does. He uses any available images of society and then says very interesting things about them.'

Wilde's wit and social comment were also perceived as a threat by some in society, as Stephen Fry points out: 'People are always suspicious that if something's funny it can't be true – the reverse is the case. In fact if something isn't funny it can't be true, because life is like that. He turned the whole picture upside down. In the microcosm of the epigram, his are often reversals of Victorian platitudes, like "Work is the curse of the drinking classes" – which is absolutely true, but is the reversal of an extremely dull Victorian remark.'

Julian Mitchell created the composite character of Lady Mount-Temple (named after a distant relative of Constance Wilde) 'to represent the attitudes of society and to show how people felt threatened by Oscar – it wasn't just the Marquess of Queensberry. Society at large was very frightened by people coming out and saying things and they thought the Empire was under threat. And actually what they didn't realise was that the Empire was doomed anyway.'

Wilde

THE CAST

Stephen Fry (Oscar Wilde) – actor, comedian, novelist, journalist, screenwriter – is a hugely versatile writer and performer, whose wit and talent were first recognised at Cambridge University, where he acted in more than thirty plays and won Edinburgh Festival Fringe awards for his writing contributions. Whilst at Cambridge, he also wrote and performed with the Footlights, the celebrated revue company, and his comedy skills were soon enlisted by the BBC, where he wrote and performed in such classic series as 'Not The Nine o'clock News', 'The Young Ones', 'Blackadder' and 'A Bit of Fry and Laurie'. He has played the imperturbable Jeeves opposite his friend and writing partner Hugh Laurie's Bertie in four series of Granada's 'Jeeves and Wooster' and has acted in a variety of films, including The Good Father, A Handful of Dust, A Fish Called Wanda, Peter's Friends, I.Q., Cold Comfort Farm, The Steal and The Wind in the Willows. His latest novel, Making History, is published by Hutchinson.

Jude Law (Bosie) began his stage career in 1993, touring Italy as Freddie in a production of Pygmalion and his theatre work has included the premieres of The Fastest Clock in the Universe and The Snow Orchid, the Royal Court revival of Live Like Pigs and the West Yorkshire Playhouse production of Death of a Salesman. He received a Tony nomination for his performance in the Broadway production of the National Theatre's Les Parents Terribles (re-titled Indiscretions), a role which, coupled with his performance as Euripedes' Ion at the Royal Shakespeare Company, saw him nominated for the Ian Charleson Award as Best Young Classical Actor. His feature film debut came with Paul Anderson's *Shopping*, followed by *I Love You, I Love You Not*, starring Jeanne Moreau. He recently completed Andrew Nichol's *Gattaca* in Los Angeles, with Ethan Hawke and Uma Thurman, which was immediately followed by 'Music From Another Room', written and directed by Charlie Peters in which he co-starred with Jennifer Tilly and Brenda Blethyn.

Vanessa Redgrave (Speranza) has long been a star of stage and screen. Daughter of Sir Michael Redgrave and Rachel Kempson, sister of Lynn and Corin and mother of actresses Natasha and Joely Richardson, she made her stage debut in 1957 and her first screen appearance the following year, playing her father's daughter in *Behind The Mask*. Following a triumphant season with the RSC in the early 1960s, she returned to films in 1966, the year in which she appeared in Antonioni's *Blow Up*, Zinnemann's *A Man For All Seasons* and Karel Reisz's *Morgan – A Suitable Case For Treatment*, for which she received an Academy Award nomination for Best Actress. She was also Oscar-nominated for *Isadora*, *Mary Queen of Scots*, *The Bostonians* and *Howard's End* and won the Academy Award for Best Supporting Actress in the title role of Fred Zinnemann's *Julia* (1977). Some of her other notable films include *Camelot*, *The Charge of The Light Brigade*, *The Devils*, *Agatha*, *Wetherby*, *A Month by The Lake* and *Mission Impossible*.

Jennifer Ehle (Constance) won the Radio Times Award for Best Newcomer as Calypso in 'The Camomile Lawn', directed by Sir Peter Hall for Britain's Channel Four. In 1996, she won the Best Actress award from the British

Academy of Film and Television Arts for her memorable portrayal of Elizabeth Bennett in 'Pride and Prejudice' on BBC Television. She has been a member of the Royal Shakespeare Company and recently played a WWII prisoner-of-war in Bruce Beresford's *Paradise Road*. She is the daughter of Rosemary Harris, Oscar-nominee for Brian Gilbert and Samuelson Productions' *Tom & Viv*.

Gemma Jones (Lady Queensberry) trained at RADA, where she won the Gold Medal in 1962. She has played numerous leading roles on stage in the West End and around the country and has been a member of both the National Theatre and the Royal Shakespeare Company. Her many memorable performances on television include the much-loved title character in the BBC's Edwardian drama serial 'The Duchess of Duke Street'. On the big screen, she has appeared in films such as Ken Russell's *The Devils*, Andrew Grieve's *On The Black Hill*, Bernard Rose's *Paperhouse*, Chris Menaul's *Feast of July* and Ang Lee's 'Sense and Sensibility'. She recently completed Sara Sugarman's Welsh comedy *Valley Girls*.

Judy Parfitt (Lady Mount-Temple) has played leading stage roles in the West End and at major theatres across the country, including a number of early appearances at the Royal Court and recently at the Aldwych in the National Theatre's presentation of *An Inspector Calls*. Amongst her many television performances, she is probably best remembered for her role in 'Jewel In The Crown', for which she received a BAFTA nomination as Best Actress. Her numerous film credits include Tony Richardson's *Hamlet*, in which she had appeared on stage, James Ivory's *Maurice*, John Irvin's

Champions, Joseph Losey's *Galileo*, Randal Kleiser's *Getting it Right*, David S. Ward's *King Ralph* and Taylor Hackford's *Dolores Claiborne*.

Michael Sheen (Robbie Ross) trained at RADA, where he won the SWET/Laurence Olivier Bursary. He made his West End debut in *When She Danced* and his stage appearances have included leading roles at Manchester's Royal Exchange Theatre, where he was nominated for the *Manchester Evening News* Award for Best Actor, and at the Royal National Theatre. In 1993, he was nominated for the Ian Charleson Award for his performance in *Don't Fool With Love*, with the Cheek By Jowl company and created the role of Fred in the world premiere of Harold Pinter's *Moonlight* at the Almeida. In 1994 he played the title role in *Peer Gynt* in Ninagawa's production is Oslo, Tokyo and London. 1996–7 has seen him play Lenny in Pinter's *The Homecoming* at the RNT. He is soon to play the title role in Ron Daniel's production of *Henry V* for the RSC to be staged later this year in Stratford, at the Barbican and a national tour. His television credits include the leading role in 'Gallowglass', a 3-part serial for the BBC. On film, he has appeared in Stephen Frears's *Mary Reilly* and Oliver Parker's *Othello*.

Zoë Wanamaker (Ada Leverson) was born in New York, daughter of actor-director Sam Wanamaker, the progenitor of London's re-created Globe Theatre. She has made countless stage appearances in London and around the United Kingdom, including seasons with the Royal Shakespeare Company and the National Theatre, in addition to playing leading roles on Broadway and in Los Angeles. Twice-nominated for the Tony Award and three times for the Laurence Olivier Award, she won New York's Drama Award for her performance in *Loot*. A frequent performer on television, she became a national favourite in Britain with her continuing role opposite Adam Faith in 'Love Hurts' for Alomo and the BBC. Here films include *Inside The Third Reich*, Tony Scott's *The Hunger* and Bob Hoskins' *The Raggedy Rawney*. She has also recently completed Beeban Kidron's *Amy Foster*.

Tom Wilkinson (Lord Queensberry) was recently seen as Pecksniff in the award-winning BBC TV series 'Martin Chuzzlewit' and his other TV work includes playing guest lead roles in 'Inspector Morse' and 'Prime Suspect', the Duke in David Thacker's production of 'Measure For Measure' as part of the BBC's Performance series, the title role in the detective series 'Resnick' and Tory Home Secretary David Hanratty in Guy Jenkin's political satire 'A Very Open Prison' and its sequel 'Crossing the Floor'. His theatre work includes the role of John Proctor in *The Crucible* at the National Theatre, *King Lear* in the West End and Doctor Stockmann in the award-winning production of *An Enemy of the People*. Amongst his films are *Sharma and Beyond*, directed by Brian Gilbert, Antonia Bird's *Priest* and Ang Lee's 'Sense and Sensibility'. He will soon be seen in Stephen Hopkins' *The Ghost and the Darkness*, Gillian Armstrong's *Oscar and Lucinda*, *The Full Monty* for Twentieth Century Fox, and this summer he plays opposite Minnie Driver in a film called *The Governess* for Parallax Pictures.

THE FILM-MAKERS

Brian Gilbert (Director) began his career in films as an actor, before spending three years at the National Film & Television School, where his graduation film, *The Devotee*, came to the attention of David Puttnam, who commissioned him to write and direct *Sharma and Beyond* for Channel Four's 'First Love' series. In 1984, he directed his first theatrical feature, *The Frog Prince*, also for Puttnam and this was followed by two successful American studio features, *Vice Versa*, starring Judge Reinhold and *Not Without My daughter*, starring Sally Field and Alfred Molina, which he also wrote. In 1994, he returned to the UK to direct the award-winning *Tom & Viv*, starring Willem Dafoe as T. S. Eliot, Miranda Richardson as his wife Vivienne Haigh-Wood and Rose-mary Harris as her mother Rose, for producers Marc and Peter Samuelson. *Tom & Viv* received two Oscar nomina-tions, two BAFTA nominations, a Golden Globe nomination and won for Best Actress at the National Board of Review.

Peter Samuelson (Producer), was educated at Cambridge University and served as production manager on *Return of the Pink Panther* and seven other feature films. He then went on to produce films including *Revenge of the Nerds* for 20th Century Fox, *A Man, A Woman and a Bank* for Embassy and

Turk 182, also for Fox. He was co-founder of Interscope Communications a leading US independent and served as its Executive Vice-President for six years. In 1990 he set up Samuelson Productions with his London-based brother, Marc Samuelson. The brothers have now made several feature films, including Tom & Viv, Dog's Best Friend, The Commissioner (in production), Playmaker and Wilde and documentaries including Man, God and Africa, Vicars, The Babe Business and Ultimate Frisbee. Tom & Viv was nominated for several awards and won the Hitchcock Prize at the Dinard Film Festival. Peter Samuelson is co-founder and serving International President of the Starlight Children's Foundation and founder/President of the Starbright Pediatric Network, which is chaired by Steven Spielberg.

Marc Samuelson (Producer) was previously Director of the UK Association of Independent Producers and of the Edinburgh International Television Festival and Managing Director of Umbrella Films, producers of White Mischief, 1984, The Playboys, Nanou and Hotel Du Paradis. In 1990 he set up Samuelson Productions with his Los Angeles-based brother Peter Samuelson. Several film and television projects are now complete, including the critically-acclaimed and Oscar-nominated film Tom & Viv, Wilde, The Commissioner (in production), Dog's Best Friend, Playmaker and documentaries Man, God and Africa, Vicars, The Babe Business and Ultimate Frisbee. Marc Samuelson chaired the principal panel of advisors to the Arts Council Of England on the investment of National Lottery finance in film production for the first year-and-half of the Arts Council's involvement. He is a director of the Starlight Children's Foundation (UK) and the Producers

Alliance for Cinema and Television and is a governor of the UK's National Film & Television School.

Julian Mitchell (Writer), was educated at Winchester and Oxford and has been a freelance writer since 1962. A prizewinning novelist and playwright, he has written copiously for television since 1966, beginning with an adaptation of his own play 'A Heritage and its History' and continuing with Somerset Maugham's 'The Alien Corn'. Among his many original plays are 'Shadow in the Sun' (Emmy, 1971) in the series 'Eliabeth R', 'A Question of Degree', 'Rust', the series 'Jennie, Lady Randolph Churchill', 'Abide With Me' (International Critics' Prize, Monte Carlo and US Humanities Award, 1977), 'The Mysterious Stranger' (Golden Eagle, 1983) nine episodes of 'Inspector Morse' (many awards and prizes) and 'Survival of the Fittest'. He has also adapted many books for television, including 'The Weather in the Streets', 'Staying On' and 'The Good Soldier'. For the cinema, he has written *Arabesque* (Stanley Donen 1965), *Another Country* (Marek Kanievska 1984), based on his own award-winning stage play, *Vincent and Theo* (Robert Altman 1990) and *August* (Anthony Hopkins 1995).

Sarah Bird (Casting Director) has cast West End theatre productions, short and feature films and television films and series such as 'Medics', 'Minder', 'Inspector Morse', 'Gallowglass', 'the Chief', 'Wycliffe', 'the Buccaneers', 'Pie in the Sky', 'Hetty Wainthrop Investigates' and 'Rhodes'. For the cinema, she has cast such films as Claude Pinoteau's *La Neige et La Feu*, Nick Ward's *Dakota Road*, Chris Menges' *Second*

Best, Nancy Meckler's *Sister My Sister* and David Drury's *Hostile Waters*.

Michael Bradsell (Editor) studied professional photography and worked on industrial and documentary films, learning camerawork, editing, scripwriting and directing before joining the BBC and becoming an editor, working on such television classics as Ken Russell's 'Isadora', Peter Watkins' 'The War Game' and 'Culloden' and Richard Cawston's 'The Royal Family'. Since becoming a freelance film editor in 1968, his credits include Ken Russell's *Women in Love*, *The Music Lovers* and *The Devils*, Michael Apted's *Stardust*, Terry Gilliam's *Jabberwocky*, Ridley Scott's *The Duellists*, Alan Clarke's *Scum*, Bill Forsyth's *Local Hero*, Pat O'Connor's 'Cal', David Drury's *Defence of the Realm*, Julian Temple's *Absolute Beginners*, Kenneth Branagh's *Henry V* and, most recently, Mark Peploe's 'Victory'.

Maria Djurkovic (Production Designer) was educated at Oxford University and won a scholarship in Theatre Design to the Riverside Theatre. As a set and costume designer, she has worked on a variety of theatre, opera and ballet productions at major theatres across the UK, including the Oxford Playhouse and the Royal Opera House. She has designed numerous familiar commercials and her work in television design includes 'Whistle Test', 'Playschool', 'The Singing Detective', 'Spender', 'Capital City' and 'Inspector Morse'. She was set dresser on Clive Donner's *Stealing Heaven* and Michael Caton Jones' *Scandal*, before becoming production designer on Benjamin Ross's *Young Poisoner's Handbook* and Curtis Radclyffe's *Sweet Angel Mine*.

Nic Ede (Costume Designer) has designed the costumes for television series such as 'The Borrowers', 'Seaforth' and 'Band of Gold' and started in feature films as a costume assistant on Fred Zinnemann's *Julia* and Warren Beatty's *Reds* and as wardrobe supervisor on Terry Jones' *Life of Brian*, Derek Jarman's *The Tempest* and Richard Attenborough's *Gandhi*. As costume designer, his films include Nicolas Roeg's *Castaway*, Bernard Rose's *Paperhouse*, Chris Menges' *A World Apart* and *Second Best*, Charles Sturridge's *A Foreign Field* and John Henderson's *Loch Ness*. In 1990 he designed the costumes for Brian Gilbert's film *Not Without My Daughter*.

Martin Fuhrer (Director of Photography) was born in Switzerland and studied at Britain's National Film and Television School in Beaconsfield. The award-winning cinematographer has worked on a number of European feature films and television productions, including the 'Eurocops' series. His first British feature was Connie Templeman's Anglo-French *Nanou* in 1985, since when he has worked on Harry Hook's *Lord of the Flies*, Fraser Heston's *City Slickers II*, for which he photographed the Bull Run sequence, Domenique Girard's *Omen IV*, Harry Hook's *The Last of His Tribe* (for which Fuhrer won the 1992 Cable Ace Award for Best Cinematography) and *Tom & Viv*, his previous collaboration with director Brian Gilbert and producers Marc and Peter Samuelson. Most recently he was director of photography for John Schelsinger on *Sweeney Todd*.

Jim Greenhorn (Sound Mixer) has worked on television series, such as 'South of the Border', 'Between the Lines', 'If You See God, Tell Him', 'Dangerous Lady' and the recent

'Emma' and 'Nostromo'. He has also recorded the sound for several films which made the transition between the small and large screen, including Anthony Minghella's *Truly, Madly, Deeply*, David Jones' *The Trial*, Antonia Bird's *Safe*, Christopher Morahan's *The Bullion Boys*, Nicolas Roeg's *Two Deaths* and John Schlesinger's *Cold Comfort Farm*. His recent cinema films include Gary Oldmans *Nil By Mouth*, David Evans *Fever Pitch* and Antonia Bird's *Face*.

Nick O'Hagan (Line Producer) has worked in various production capacities in film and television. As production co-ordinator, he worked on James Ivory's *Howard's End*, the television dramas 'The Man Who Cried' and 'An Exchange of Fire' and on the series 'Press Gang' and 'Class Act'. He was associate producer of the film *Solitaire For Two*, production manager on the television series 'She's Out' and production supervisor on Hetty Macdonald's critically-praised film *Beautiful Thing*. Most recently, he acted as line producer on David Evans' film of Nick Hornby's *Fever Pitch*.

Debbie Wiseman (Composer) has composed over 70 scores for film and television including *Tom & Viv*, *Haunted*, *The Dying of the Light*, *The Missing Postman*, *The Good Guys*, *The Upper Hand*, *Female Perversions*, *A Week in Politics*, *Children's Hospital*, *The Churchills*, *The People's Century*, *Little Napoleons*, *Death of Yugoslavia*, *Shrinks*, *It Might Be You*, *Making Babies* and *Loved by You*.

Debbie has won and been nominated for numerous awards including Winner of Theme Music of the Year for *The Good Guys* in the 1993 Television & Radio Industry Club Awards, and Winner of Best Original Theme Music 1991 for *Shrinks* in the Silents to Satellite Awards. Debbie was nominated for the Rank Film Laboratories Award for

Creative Originality in The Carlton Television Women in Film Awards 1994 and nominated for Best Commissioned Score in the 1995 Ivor Novello Awards and the Royal Television Society Awards for *Death of Yugoslavia*.

CAST & CREDITS

Oscar Wilde	Stephen Fry
Lord Alfred Douglas	Jude Law
Lady 'Speranza' Wilde	Vanessa Redgrave
Constance Wilde	Jennifer Ehle
Lady Queensberry	Gemma Jones
Lady Mount-Temple	Judy Parfitt
Robert Ross	Michael Sheen
Ada Leverson	Zoë Wanamaker
The Marquess of Queensberry	Tom Wilkinson
John Gray	Ioan Gruffud
Lionel Johnson	Matthew Mills
Ernest Dowson	Jason Morell
Charles Gill	Peter Barkworth
C. O. Humphreys	Robert Lang
Judge	Philip Locke
Edward Carson	David Westhead
Cyril Wilde	Jack Knight
Cyril Wilde, aged 4	Jackson Leach
Vyvyan Wilde	Laurence Owen
Alfred Wood	Benedict Sandiford
Charles Parker	Mark Letheren

Alfred Taylor	Michael Fitzgerald
Rentboy	Orlando Bloom
Mine Owner	Bob Sessions
Jones	Adam Garcia
First Miner	Joseph May
Second Friend	Jamie Leene
First Friend	James D'Arcy
Undergraduate	Orlando Wells
George Alexander	Robin Kermode
Lady Bracknell	Avril Elgar
Miss Prism	Jean Ainslie
Algernon	Andrew Havill
Gwendolen	Biddy Hodson
Mrs Allonby	Judi Maynard
Chasuble	Hugh Munro
Lord Illingworth	Michael Simkins
Hotel Manager	James Vaughan
Head Waiter	Richard Cubison
Nanny	Christine Moore
Warder	John Bleasdale
Detective	Peter Forbes
Doorman at the Cadogan	Peter Harding
Cabman	Edward Laurie
Policeman	Geoffrey Leesley
Prison Officer	Colin Maclachlan
Waiter	Simon Molloy
Reporter	Hywel Simons
Arthur	Albert Welling
Doorkeeper	Arthur Whybrow

MAIN UNIT

Assistant Producer	Rachel Cuperman
Production Co-ordinator	Fiona Weir
Assistant Production Co-ordinator	Harry Teacher
Producer's Assistant (US)	Pam Oseransky
Production Assistants	Edward Mitchell
	Ian Thomson
Production Office Assistant	Linzi Baltrunas
Production Department Trainees	Ginny Gilbert
	Pamela Samuelson
Location Managers	Rachel Neale
	Amanda Stevens
Head of Security	Fred Kelly
Unit Manager	Marilla Elliott
Fist Assistant Director	Cordelia Hardy
Second Assistant Director	Toby Sherborne
Third Assistant Director	Andrew Woodhead
Floor Runner	Melanie Bägust
Additional Assistant Director	Alexa Hester
Runners	George Lamb
	Leonard Samuelson
Camera Operator	Mike Miller
Focus Puller	Sam Garwood
Clapper Loader	Sarah Bartles-Smith
Camera Grip	Darren Quinn
Additional Camera Operators	Richard Philpot
	Philip Sindall
	Steve Parker
	Ben Davis
Additional Focus Pullers	Daniel Cohen

	Steven Hall
	Keith Thomas
	Chris Pinnock
Additional Clapper Loader	Andy Newall
Technocrane Operator	John Murray
Additional Crane Operator	Paul Legal
Additional Grips	Nick Pearson
	Kirk Thornton
	Keith Manning
	Andrew Edridge
FT2 Camera Trainees	Jane Dobson
	Jake Hull
Script Supervisor	Liz West
Boom Operator	Simon Firsht
FT2 Sound Assistant	Stephen Mayer
Chief Make-Up Artist	Pat Hay
Chief Hair Dresser	Stephen Rose
Make-Up Artist	Helen Johnson
Hair Dressers	Liz Michie
	Gerry Jones
Art Director	Martyn John
Stand-By Art Director	Sarah Hauldren
Assistant Art Director	Keith Slote
Production Buyer	Judy Ducker
Assistant Production Buyer	Tanya Bowd
Art Department Assistants	Caireen Todd
	Lucinda Thomson
Art Department Trainees	Liliana Cifonelli
	Luke Smith

Prop Master	Mike Power
Chargehand Props	Nigel Salter
Dressing Props	Patrick Black
	Chris Cutler
	Rob McArthur
	John Gooch
	Dean Humphrey
	Tom Playdell-Pearce
Stand-By Props	Roger Edwards
	Noel Cowell
Special Effects	Bob Hollow
Road Surfacing	Gary Plumley
Props Drivers	Jim Hall
	Nick Curson
Assistant Costume Designer	Camilla Fiddian-Green
Costume Supervisor	Ali Goss
Costume Assistant	Miles Johnson
Additional Costume	Melissa Layton
Production Accountant	Patrick Isherwood
Assistant Accountant	Rachel Quigley Smith
Cashier	Douglas Isherwood
Accountant (US)	Saryl Hirsch
Post Production Supervisor	John Kay
First Assistant Editor	Daryl Jordan
Second Assistant Editor	John Nuth
FT2 Trainee Assistant Editor	David King
FT2 Trainee Assistant Editor	Shani Duncan
Post-Production Runner	Neil Stevens
Supervising Sound Editor	Colin Miller AMPS

Dialogue Editor	Stefan Henrix
Foley Editor	Martin Cantwell
Assistant Sound Editor	James Boyle
ADR Voice Casting	Louis Elman
Colour Grader	Clive Noakes
Unit Pubicist	Graham Smith
Stills Photographer	Liam Daniel
Script Co-ordinator	Nicky Ryde
US Casting	Donald Paul Pemrick
Casting Assistant	Julia Gale
Chaperones	Audrey Knight
	Heather Owen
	Janet Ellis
Unit Nurse/Rigger	Jordan Archer
Gaffer	Larry Prinz
Best Boy	Tony Devlin
Electricians	Martin Cox
	Terry Eden
	Paul Kelly
	Cameron 'Fred' Todd
	Michael O'Connell
Practical Electrician	Richard Stevens
Additional Best Boy	Roger Lowe
Construction Manager	Michael Boleyn
Construction Team	Sarah Crawford
	David Chettleborough
	Steven Wilson
	Clare Holland
	Jim Dyson

	Robert Weller
	Ray McNeil
	Brian Dowling
	Steve Lazarides
	Stewart Watson
	Robert Brown
Construction Buyer (Spain)	Annette Powell
Construction Transport (Spain)	Michael O'Shea
Stand-By Carpenter	Dave Coley
Stand-By Painter	Peter Wilkinson
Stand-By Rigger	John Weller
Unit Drivers	Barry Leonti
	Len Furssedonn
	Melvin Kiernan
Minibus Drivers	Steve Bignell
	Dean Samain
	Gary Preston
	Jeff Rowe
Transport Captain	Mickey Webb
Facility Drivers	Paul Webb
	Donna Webb
	Darren Nye
	Mickey Finnegan
	David Nye
	Gary Lord
	Ron Allett
	Les Allett
	Dave Russell
	Adam Driver-Williams
Catering Crew	Jack Gosik

Turnabay Daniels
Karen Woods

SPANISH UNIT

Unit Production Manager	Gilly Case
Production Manager	Mark Albela
Production Secretary	Anna Cassina
Location Manager	Julio Fernández
Production Accountant	Beatriz Calvo
Second Assistant Director	Manolo Santa Cruz
Third Assistant Director	Rodrigo Ruiz
Floor Runner	Salvador Yagüe
Camera Operator	Joan Benet
Focus Puller	Marc Beneria
Prop Buyer	Carola Angulo
Additional Make-up	Sandra Mundi
	Eugenio Bagaglia
Additional Hair	Arrate Garmendia
	Saturnino Merino
Costume Assistants	Angela Dodson Oxley
	Pilar Sainz de Vicuña
Driver/Runners	Jose Manuel Villa Cortes
	Fernando Matas García
	Jaime Garcia Lopez
Electricians	Victor Santos
	Jose Llopart
Grip	Raimon Buficidit
	Antonio Llopart
Crane Truck Driver	German Olariaga
Local Runner	Fernando Olmo
Location Guard	Daniel Lopez

	Joaquin Francisco Hernandez
Local Assistants	Jesus Enrique Molina
	David Mejia Quiros
	Luis Jeronimo Miranda
	Jose Manuel Flores
Accounting Services	Foster Lewis Stone
	Shipleys
Airline Services	American Airlines
Anamorphic Lenses	2.35 Research
Banking Services	Barclays Bank, Soho Square
Camera Consumables	The Film Game
Catering	Woodhall Catering
Chauffeur Services	The Car Service
Cherry Picker and Scissor Lifts	EPL Plant and Access Hire
Colour	Rank Film Laboratories
Completion Guarantor	Film Finances
Costumes	Angels & Bermans
Crockery	Spode China
	Waterford Wedgwood Retail
Crowd Casting	Ray Knight Casting
Digital Sound Editing Facilities	The Sound Design Company
Editing Facilities	Salon Productions
Facility Vehicles	Mickey Webb Transport
Film Processing	Metrocolour London
Financial Services	Guinness Mahon & Co
Florist	Wild at Heart

Freight Services	Samfreight
Grip Equipment and Cranes	Grip House
Horses and Carriages	Debbie Kaye
Insurance Services	Near North Entertainment
Legal Services	Olswang
Lighting Equipment	Michael Samuelson Lighting
Marketing and Promotional Services	The Creative Partnership
Minibuses	Wheels in Motion
Moviecam Compact Cameras	Sammy's
Negative Cutter	Sylvia Wheeler Film Services
Opticals	General Screen Enterprises
Oscar's Jewllery	Lynda Perkin at Antiquarius
Post Production Facilities	Shepperton Studios
Prop Pick-Up	Gee Whizz Transport
Public Relations	Dennis Davidson Associates
Sound Equipment	Richmond Film Services
Spanish Production Services	KanZaman S.A.
Titles Design	Cine Image
Travel Services	Screen & Music Travel
Walkie-Talkies	Wavevend Radio Communications
Wallcoverings	Sandersons
Web Site	Demon Internet

Wig Supplies

Wig Specialities
London & New York
Wig Company

Originated on Motion Picture Film from Kodak.

SAMMY'S   ANGELS   MICHAEL SAMUELSON
                                                 LIGHTING

The Producers would like to thank the following for their invaluable contribution to the film:

Nick Adams   Christopher Fowler   Nigel Palmer
Maggie Anderson   Dennis Fraser   Andrew Patrick
Tim Angel   Mark Furssedonn   Aline Perry
Kim Ballard   Sue Gilbert   Lord Queensberry
Jane Barclay   Lorraine Hamilton   John Rendall
Bill Barringer   Sharon Harel   Mindy Richmond
Deborah Blackburn   Nick Harris   Teresa Rogers
David Bouchier   Merlin Holland   David Rubinson
Len Brown   Alan Hopper   Geoff Salmon
Reinhard Brundig   Anthony Jones   Michael Samuelson
Richard Burridge   Miles Ketley   Sir Sydney Samuelson
Sally Caplan   Carolyn Lambert   David Scott
James Coates   Shirley Lavis   Colin Sherborne
Sheila Colman   Hannah Leader   James Shirras
Mark Deitch   Martin Lewis   Michael Shyjka
Mike Devry   Annie Littleton   Peter Smith
Eddie Dias   Julie McCarron   Steven Soloway
Joe Dunton   Barry Measure   Judy Szucs
Graham Easton   Jane Moore   Stewart Till
Lucy Ellmann   Peter Nahum   Derek Townshend
David Elstein   Jeremy Newton   James Weld
Sarah Fforde   Andy Ordonez   David Wilder
                                                   Kate Wilson

and would particularly like to thank the following without whom this film would not have been made:

Simon Perry   Premila Hoon   Lisbeth Savill

The Producers would like to thank the owners of the following locations for their co-operation:

Excmo Ayuntamiento de Granada, Emucesa
Honourable Society of The Middle Temple, Lincoln's Inn
Hospital Universitario Virgen de las Nieves
Houghton Lodge, Stockbridge
Knebworth
The Liberal Club
Luton Hoo
National Trust
Magdalen College, Oxford
Oxford Prison
Royal Parks
Somerset House ·
Swanage Pier
and the British Flm Commission

Produced in association with Wall-to-Wall Television Ltd.

Soundtrack album available on MCI Records.

Music Recordist	Dick Lewzey
Recorded at	Abbey Road Studios
Mixed at	CTS Studios
Orchestra Leader	Perry Montague-Mason
Strings Co-ordinator	Justin Pearson
Score Orchestrator	Debbie Wiseman

Music Consultant   Roz Colls

Music Preparation   Tony Wharmby

"AH, LEAVE ME NOT TO PINE" from *The Pirates of Penzance*
Words and Music by Gilbert & Sullivan

DOLBY STEREO

Screenplay and novelisation available from Dove Books, Dove Audio and Orion Media and Orion Books.

'In Summer' and 'Two Loves' by Lord Alfred Douglas by kind permission of Mrs Sheila Colman.

Developed with the assistance of British Screen Finance Ltd, London, England and the support of the European Script Fund, an initiative of the MEDIA Programme of the Commission of the European Communities.

Supported by the National Lottery through The Arts Council of England.

Banking finance provided by Guinness Mahon & Co Ltd.

Filmed on location in Oxford, Dorset and London, England, in Spain and at Grip House Studios, Greenford.

www.oscarwilde.com

MPAA No. 35250